THE
CRUCIFIX

Naomi Cashman

A catalogue record for this book is available from the National Library of Australia

Disclaimer

This is a work of fiction. Names, characters, places, incidents and events, other than those clearly in the public domain, are fictitious and any resemblance to actual persons, living or dead, is entirely coincidental.

To my partner and greatest supporter
and to all the yesterdays that led us to today.

Author's Note

This story is inspired by the real-life setting of the Convent of Mercy in Cobh, Ireland.

Prologue

'Come on, quickly! Come in before you get soaked from the rain. Apologies, we're running a little behind schedule; we're just waiting for one more couple to arrive and then we'll begin the tour. How's everyone keeping? Where are you all from?'

At the guide's words, Malcolm headed directly to the dying fire nearby, trying to keep himself warm as he stood in the draughty, makeshift living room. He assumed the room had once been a drawing room for some of the more senior nuns, given how expansive it was. There were large windows to the right, overlooking the cathedral at the front of the building and to the harbour in the distance. The gaudy, ornate marble fireplace sat in the middle of the room. The carpet, now faded, may have been a rich red colour once – far too grand for anyone other than a senior nun. To Malcolm, the whole room just appeared sad and outdated. A few plastic fold-out chairs were the only items of furniture in the room bar a pitiful, self-crafted coffee station accompanied by a few milk jugs with unappetising items floating in them. The large windows were murky and cracking, allowing the cold night air to enter, while black mould festered in the corners of the room.

Malcom sighed. Out of all the nights that she could have dragged him out, his mother had chosen tonight, the most miserable night they'd seen in October. And for what? To bring him to this decaying cesspool for *fun*? He couldn't remember the last time the weather had been this bad. The rain was torrential, causing flooding in the streets, and trees had collapsed beneath the gale-force winds. And his mother had decided that a tour of a convent next to the sea would be a great activity for them both to do! He shook his head and rubbed his hands together, blowing into them to try to get some heat circulating.

Across the room, his pathetic, eager-eyed mother was talking animatedly with the tour guide, while nursing a cup of weak black coffee. Malcolm snorted. *She doesn't even like the taste of coffee*, he thought. She always said it was too bitter. Most likely, she had only taken the cup because everyone else had leapt at the invitation of a free hot drink.

Malcom rolled his eyes and turned to face the fire, focusing on the dancing flames and the crackling of the wood. His mother lived for this sort of thing. She loved to visit any old building with a gruesome history that was within a five-mile radius. Usually, he talked his way out of going with her, but his recent suspension from school and the string of warnings from the police meant that he was supposed to be under her constant watch. She didn't trust him to be on his own in case he 'acted out again', so he had no choice but to be on his best behaviour. He hated the fact that his every move was constantly scrutinised. And he hadn't even done anything to warrant being treated like a prisoner. It was his friends who had made the bad decisions, not him. It wasn't his idea to lock the new kid in one of the lockers. He had just happened to be there. And when he was called to the principal's office, he wasn't about to snitch on his friends. Unfortunately, his silence was taken as an admission of guilt, and he was lumped with the same punishment – suspended for the next two weeks. *Not much of a punishment*, he thought, smirking, before his expression darkened once more as he gazed into the flames.

He was distracted from his thoughts by a sharp pinch on the exposed skin on the back of his neck and his mother's harsh voice in his ear.

'We talked about this, Malcom,' she half-whispered through gritted teeth. 'You promised me that you would behave. Please, for the love of God, for the sake of one night, can you try to put a smile on your face and suck it up? I know you don't want to be here. You've made that crystal clear, but if you could just get over yourself for a few minutes, you might even learn something while you're here.'

Malcolm glanced up at her from under his eyelashes. *Here we go again*, he thought. He opened his mouth to stop the anticipated lecture, but she continued to speak, ignoring anything he had to say as usual. 'You know, no one even knows what happened to her,' she said quietly, leaning in closer to him. 'The string of murders just stopped, and it's like she fell off the face of the earth. She just disappeared, never to be seen again. No further records have ever been found. Isn't that just insane? I mean, it's as if …'

'Who disappeared, Mom? What are you even talking about?'

'Sister Katherine, of course. Who else would I be talking about?' She grabbed his arm and squeezed it hard, dragging him closer still. 'And you know what's creepy about the whole thing?' she asked.

He could feel her breath on his face, could practically taste the bitter coffee that she had downed only a few moments ago. 'What's that, Mom?' Malcom said in monotone.

'The crucifix disappeared too, without a trace, so the cursed object could just be walking around this very town.'

'What crucifix are you talking about? A crucifix wouldn't be able to walk, Mother. Don't be stupid!'

His mother glared at him. Malcolm's blood ran cold. He wanted to shrink back into his hoodie.

'You know what I mean, Malcolm. Come on now, the tour is just starting.'

The group trudged up the creaky wooden stairs, swatting their way through the cascade of century-old cobwebs that adorned every crevice of the place.

This is disgusting, Malcolm thought. *You'd think they would've made an effort to clean the place.* He swiped at his face, trying to remove an invisible web.

After they had passed by a series of cramped, musty-smelling bedrooms, the guide asked them to gather in the narrow hallway to give them the next set of ominous facts. Malcom thought he must have been new to the job. The young man fumbled with his handwritten notes and sweat beaded his forehead despite the cold. The whole thing was quite comical.

'Right here, ladies and gentlemen, is the dorm room that Sister Katherine occupied right up until she became the Reverend Mother of the orphanage,' the guide said, gesturing towards the room. 'She was the very last person to ever occupy this room. Our records show that some of the orphans were terrified because of the strange events that used to take place here. They refused to reside in it, fearful that the Devil would notice them, so the room was never used by anyone else up until the closure of the orphanage over a hundred years ago. It has remained untouched since that evil night when she allowed her nefarious tendencies to take control. Please feel free to take a wander around the room … if you dare.'

Malcolm rolled his eyes at the tour guide's weak attempt to create a frightening atmosphere and pushed past a few people to see inside the room for himself. It looked just like every other room in the dormitory he had passed by. Mostly bare and with very little furniture. He couldn't understand why everyone was falling over each other to try and take a photograph of the empty interior.

The excited chatter from the tour group irritated Malcom, so he decided to clarify why everyone was losing their minds. 'So, what was the deal with this nun? She went mad and killed a few kids, was that it?'

The rest of the group stopped their conversations short, eager to hear the dark tales of the notorious woman.

'Malcolm!' his mother whispered, her face flushed. 'Don't interrupt the man.'

'No, no, it is quite alright,' said the guide with a subdued smile. 'Many people don't know the story of Sister Katherine's life. You're right. She murdered the children who were in her care. Brutally and viciously. She was a woman completely without mercy. Some statements we found in the notebooks written by a local priest named Father Michael suggest that Sister Katherine wasn't exactly "human".' The tour guide flexed his fingers in the air in awkward air quotes. 'It's been said that she became obsessed with the idea of owning the crucifix and, when she attempted to steal it for herself, a vicious darkness came over her and completely transformed her from the woman that everyone knew. There are many speculations as to whether this woman was clinically insane, but most of our records suggest that those around her believed the crucifix she coveted was cursed by the Devil himself. Willing to commit a most grievous sin to obtain it, she fell into the hands of the Devil, totally transforming her into a creature of darkness.'

Malcom laughed in disbelief. He couldn't help it; it all sounded too far-fetched. He had seen too many horror films to be unable to pick out a bad story line when he heard one.

The guide nodded in understanding. 'It's difficult to believe, I know. I didn't quite trust it myself at first.' He grabbed a nearby chair, dusted it off with a tissue that he pulled from his coat sleeve and slumped down into it. 'Let me tell you the full story.'

I

1865

As the rickety horse and trap rounded the narrow bend, the Convent of Mercy slowly came into view. The dark and gloomy November sky did nothing to help the appearance of the dilapidated convent. The windows were caked with dirt and enclosed by iron bars, as if trapping everyone inside like a prison. The crucifix, which stood at the top of the building, cast an ominous shadow across the lawn, demanding the attention of everyone in the vicinity. There was a row of religious stone statues overlooking the cathedral in the distance. Katherine recognised one of them as being Mary, the Virgin Mother. The original white paint of the statues was now dull, almost grey in colour, and was peeling from age around the centre of the faces. The distortion of the facial features made the figures almost unrecognisable and filled Katherine with a sense of unease as she looked up at them. She imagined that if statues were able to feel anything, the sheer pain from the cracked faces would've been unbearable.

She took a deep breath and looked around, trying to accept that this bleak place would be her home from now on.

She had heard whispers in her village about this convent. This was the place to which all orphaned, troubled and misunderstood souls were discarded when no one knew what to do with them. The convent kept them out of sight and away from the prying eyes of the nosy villagers. They were placed into God's hands to allow their faith to show them the righteous path. At least, that's what she had heard. She'd known it had been only a matter of time before she would be forcibly sent there. Her mother, unable to accept her for who she truly was, had threatened her with it ever since she'd turned fourteen. She would call Katherine obstinate and deceptive, traits she found abhorrent. Katherine reflected on the few notable incidents that she'd been involved in where some people had got hurt, but that had been unavoidable. And of course she'd told the odd lie here and there, but who hasn't? She wasn't perfect, but nor was she a troubled soul who needed to be saved.

She sighed, then focused on her surroundings. She believed coming here was her destiny, but not so soon, nor because she'd become an orphan.

She understood why people had once commented on the grandeur of the building. With the extensive grounds overlooking the town's harbour and the convent's wide arched gothic entrances and oriel windows, one could imagine the convent as an appealing place, one that Katherine wouldn't have minded being sent to. Now it was a different story.

Katherine pulled her threadbare shawl closer around her body. A futile attempt to try and keep some heat in her body, but the bitterly cold sea air made retaining any warmth impossible. The trap shuddered to an abrupt halt at the top of the steep hill, rolling back a few inches before the horse steadied himself. She took a breath, braced herself and gingerly stepped down from the carriage, clutching her tattered case. A priest greeted her with a nod of his head and reached out to take her case from her but offered no words of comfort.

The sharp wind slapped her in the face like knives, and she had to fight to keep her hair from winding its way around her neck. She glanced around, her eyes darting in every direction, trying to take in the unsettling surroundings.

The sudden sound of sharp heels clacking against the stone staircase at the entrance of the building drew her attention. Descending from the stairs, was the tall, domineering figure of a young nun with her head held high. Katherine guessed from the woman's confident steps and the pristine stiff habit that she wore that this was the Reverend Mother. She must've been in her early thirties at most, with dark, angular eyes that focused on Katherine with a piercing gaze. Her sharp features stood out against her pale, almost translucent skin. A shining gold crucifix hung on a chain around her neck and Katherine couldn't help but stare. Its grandeur was dazzling. It appeared to be double-plated, with thick, curved lines forming the shape of the cross and red jewels adorning the exterior.

Katherine thought this was odd. She had never come across a nun who would be so brazen and expose skin on their neck to showcase such an ostentatious item before. Normally, they wore the same simple, understated chain concealed beneath their habit, lest one be deemed vain. Why would she be wearing something so ornate? After she thrashed out this idea for a few moments, she brushed her confusion off. Perhaps a Reverend Mother was awarded more liberties, or maybe there were different rules for nuns in bigger towns. A wisp of dark hair had managed to escape from underneath the nun's veil. She had yet to utter a single word. Katherine stood in front of her, shaking as the nun scrutinised every inch of her.

Katherine shuffled her feet in the awkwardness of the eerie silence. Ever since her parents' funeral a few weeks ago, everyone she came across had just stared at her. She hated it. She hated the deep pity in their eyes. She didn't want sympathy from anyone, and the silence from the nun reminded her of that dark time. She coughed into her hands and forced herself to look up and meet the nun's eyes. What she saw there made her stomach drop and her cough died in her throat, almost as quickly as it had begun. An involuntary shudder racked its way through her body. There was something about the young nun's eyes – their darkness and the vast emptiness – that rattled Katherine to the bone. She had a gift for reading people, and she suspected this woman was someone to be feared.

Finally, the nun spoke. 'Welcome, child, I'm Sister Nora.' Her smile was forced as she folded her arms across her chest.

Katherine was surprised that her voice didn't sound like it belonged to her body. Given how young she looked, she had expected her voice to be soft and gentle, but there was a distinct guttural rasp to it, reminding Katherine of the time she had been forced to try her father's pipe.

The incident had occurred late in the evening at her Uncle John's wake when the men were red-faced and blustering from drinking too much bootleg whiskey. The musty smell of smoke and aged sweat from men long overdue for a bath had invaded Katherine's senses. In the last few hours, she had endured the tiresome charade of the men attempting to play the bodhrán and tin whistle as a way of 'honouring' John. She kept asking her mother if she could be excused, but each time her mother had shushed her and barked at her to 'Show some respect for the dead'. After a while the men, having grown tired of their musical session, moved on to the whole process of smoking their pipes. Her father, Dermot, spied Katherine in the corner with her sullen face and thought it would be funny if 'his little Kathy' had a turn. Despite her mother's somewhat weak protests, Dermot was adamant as 'head of the house' that he was to be obeyed, a sentiment wholeheartedly backed up by the remainder of the drunken fools in the room.

Having no choice in the matter, Katherine took the pipe from her father's outstretched hand while everyone looked on in glee, nudging each other as if it was the most interesting thing they had seen in years. It was only after Katherine had inhaled the thick, earthy tobacco that she realised why they found the thought of her smoking it so amusing. Her chest heaved and she coughed and spluttered as the smoke escaped from her mouth in short bursts. She thrust the pipe back to her father, who was bent double with laughter, then ran for a cup of water to wash away the taste. Her throat ached for days after, and she would never forget the raspy timbre of her voice.

The sound of Sister Nora clearing her throat brought her back to her depressing reality.

'I do so hope that you'll feel at home here. Our routine may appear somewhat … unorthodox at first, but don't worry, I'm confident that you will adapt soon enough, as all our children have.'

Her gaze shifted to Father Michael in front of her. 'Thank you, Father Michael, you can go now.'

It appeared as if Father Michael was well used to the ways of Sister Nora as he gave her a curt nod in acknowledgement of his dismissal. Katherine thought he was in his sixties, but his morose demeanour made it difficult to guess his true age. His face was deeply creased, giving the impression that he held much pain and sadness.

The priest placed her case at her feet. He squinted at Katherine with a deep frown before shuffling towards the chapel that stood next to the orphanage.

As Father Michael climbed the stairs at the entrance to the chapel, he glanced over his shoulder, sneaking a look back at the pair. Sister Nora was standing directly in front of the young orphan. Katherine cowered with fear as she craned her neck to look up at the intimidating nun in front of her. The poor child had no idea of her fate; none of the children did.

It didn't use to be like this, he thought as he entered his office at the back of the chapel and lit a nearby candle.

The convent used to be a place where lost souls would find the righteous path and become whole again. But now it was shrouded in a malevolent darkness. A strong presence of evil emanated from within Sister Nora, and he sensed it was growing more powerful as the years went by.

As he sat down at his writing desk, he dropped his head into his hands in resignation. He longed for the young Nora who he had grown fond of when she was first being trained in the sisterhood. She had been warm and bubbly; the type of woman he could confide in. If there was ever a problem, she volunteered immediately to help. She took great pride in her work and was dedicated in her preparation to give herself fully to the Lord, focusing solely on completing her training. He thought about one time when they'd been working in the communal garden together on a crisp autumn evening. Their hands were blue and numb with the cold and, despite how eager Father Michael had been to postpone the work until the weather improved, Sister Nora would have none of it. She insisted, with a smile on her face, that they were helping the less fortunate by providing them with the produce from their hard work, so they must find the strength to persist. She even suggested that if they worked faster, they wouldn't feel the cold as much. He missed that Sister Nora; the Nora who was his friend. But that woman was long gone. Her body might still be there, but her soul had died long ago. An empty vessel occupied by a dark force remained in her place. He reached deep into his pocket and pulled out his string of rosary beads and prayed with all his might for the soul of the woman he once knew and loved.

II

Father Michael's sudden departure meant Katherine was alone with Sister Nora in the front garden. She opened her mouth to speak but Sister Nora cut her off.

'You may only speak when spoken to,' she said, then briskly turned on her heels and beckoned Katherine to follow her through the darkness into the orphanage.

Much to Katherine's dismay, the inside of the building was no better than its grim exterior. The corridors were draughty and the walls were wet from condensation due to the lack of proper ventilation. There were a few faded photographs hanging on the walls, along with some moth-eaten tapestries. The ragged fabric made the symbols that were sewn on them difficult to decipher, but she managed to recognise the crossed keys of the disciple Peter on one of them. *Why bother even hanging them up*, she thought, *if they're so worn you don't even know what you're looking at?*

Sister Nora led her through a narrow stone corridor, passing several children who were hard at work with dusters and wet rags, removing cobwebs and grime from the pictures and walls. They kept their eyes lowered, focused on their chores.

Most of the children were covered in dust and dirt themselves and their faces were an alarming shade of grey, as if they hadn't washed themselves in months. None of them attempted to offer her a comforting smile or a greeting, making her feel even more apprehensive about what her life was going to be like here.

Sister Nora led Katherine by weak candlelight up a winding wooden staircase to her room which was to be her 'home' for the next few years. The miniscule candle flickered, creating monstrous shadows on the walls that Katherine imagined were trying to reach out and devour them. Swallowing her fear, she kept her eyes firmly on the floorboards, trying not to focus on the eerie surroundings. Eventually, after what felt like an eternity, they arrived at a small open door.

'This is your room,' Sister Nora said with a brief jerk of her head, gesturing for Katherine to proceed inside.

The room itself was dingy and sparsely furnished. It smelt stale, as if it had been quite some time since someone had last stepped foot in there. The wooden floorboards were quite aged and creaked under the strain of each movement, threatening to give way beneath her. The only furniture in the room were two narrow single beds on each side, a thin moss-green blanket and small writing desk against the wall on the right-hand side.

Katherine gripped her case tightly as she stepped into the room. She swept her hand across the blanket on the bed. The coarse fibres sent a shiver down her spine. The window on the far side of the room was covered in a mixture of dust and condensation that had developed into a thick layer of grime. She tugged the sleeve of her dress over her hand and wiped it across the window so she could gaze out. She wondered if she'd be able to see the cathedral spire in the town on a less foggy day.

Sister Nora had stood silently on the threshold of the door while Katherine took in her minimal surroundings. Now, from the corner of her eye, Katherine noticed the nun seemed agitated. She fiddled with the crucifix around her neck and kept clenching her jaw, as if she was in pain, but her face remained unchanged. Uncertain how to react to the nun's strange behaviour, Katherine turned back to the bleak scene outside her window. She noticed for the first time a small, gothic graveyard adjacent to her room. A ripple of fear swept through her at the thought of sleeping next to a graveyard.

She jumped when Sister Nora suddenly appeared beside her, leaned down and whispered in her ear, 'You know, none of our forsaken children ever truly leave us.'

The woman's breath was icy against the skin on Katherine's neck, and she shuddered. She glanced at the nun and frowned, puzzled by the absurdity of her words, but Sister Nora's attention was focused on the caretaker outside, who was struggling with a battered wheelbarrow covered by a dark tarp.

As Katherine watched, the blood drained from her face. A small, pale hand dangled over the side of the wheelbarrow. That was why the caretaker had been exerting so much effort – he was moving a body! Desperate to get away from the horror of what she had just witnessed, Katherine backed away from the window. She could barely muster the courage to glance at Sister Nora, who had made her way back to the door. The nun's nonchalance terrified Katherine, and she was too afraid to speak.

Sister Nora smirked. 'Our children never leave us,' she reiterated before slamming the door behind her.

What sort of nefarious place is this? Katherine thought as she slumped down on her bed in despair.

III

Later that evening, after what felt like a lifetime, Katherine was pulled from her tumultuous thoughts by the sound of a shrill bell ringing. She quickly rose from the bed, cracked open the door and peered outside to see where the noise was coming from. All the orphans were moving in unison towards the staircase. One of the young girls jerked Katherine into the line next to her.

'We're meant to head down to the dining room for dinner when the bell rings,' she whispered. 'My name is Rose, by the way; you can sit next to me if you like.'

Katherine smiled in gratitude as she quickly fell into step with the rest of the orphans. She glanced over at Rose, trying to guess her age. Her willowy physique and sunken face made it difficult to gauge how old she was, but she thought she must have been a little younger than herself, perhaps around twelve years old. Her matted blonde hair lay in a tousled mess on top of her head, as if it hadn't been combed in years. Katherine noticed some faded red marks on her forearm and wondered what had happened to her.

Rose must have caught her gaze because she tugged the sleeve of her frock down to cover the marks. She looked up at Katherine, her blue eyes wide with alarm, and offered her a nervous smile, as if to say, 'Don't worry about it'. Katherine managed to curl her lips into a forced grimace in return. Those marks on Rose's arm told a story which they couldn't talk about now, but Katherine was determined to find out the reason for them.

The girls descended into the dining room, their movements almost robotic as each girl moved with purpose to stand behind the bench seats. They waited in silence, eyes downcast, hands clasped behind their backs. The air was thick with apprehension.

A few minutes later, following the delicate chime of a bell, the heavy double doors of the room opened once again and in marched a procession of nuns. Their black habits bustled with each step as they made their way to the head table at the front of the room. None of the nuns glanced at any of the children. Their faces were equally as stoic and unmoving as Sister Nora's, but Katherine had noticed one nun, who seemed older than the rest, heave her shoulders as if she'd been holding her breath. She glanced up and caught Katherine's eyes for a fleeting moment as she moved forward. This nun appeared different from the rest; her movements were slower and more hesitant. Her face was quite personable, and there were smile lines on her face, but her eyes held such a vast amount of fear that Katherine herself became nervous. She quickly dropped her gaze and looked down.

Once the nuns were seated, the orphans were permitted to sit. Sister Nora, who swept in at the back of the procession, squinted at each child as she floated up to the head table and sat down in the vacant seat in the middle. She raised her right hand and, as if on auto pilot, the orphans began to say grace.

'Bless us, O Lord, and these thy gifts which we are about to receive from thy bounty. Through Christ, our Lord, Amen.'

As soon as they were finished saying grace, Sister Nora once again raised her hand and everyone but Katherine began to devour the questionable meal that had been placed in front of them. Katherine eyed the thick, muddy mixture of grey meat and limp vegetables with distaste. The thought of eating it made her feel nauseous. She gazed around the room until her eyes landed on the top table. Like the orphans, every nun was silent, eyes focused on their bowls. All except one.

Sister Nora sat staring blankly into space as she clutched the crucifix around her neck. As she pulled on the crucifix, the chain moved, revealing puckered, jagged red lines marking the skin beneath. Katherine gasped. The wound looked excruciating, but Sister Nora showed no hint of pain, even though the more she pulled on the chain, the deeper the injury she was causing herself.

As Katerine watched, Sister Nora's pulling action escalated, becoming erratic. She appeared to have trouble breathing, and beads of sweat began to form on her forehead.

Katherine looked around her in disbelief. None of the girls took any notice; they were too concerned with finishing their own meals. She wanted to scream at Sister Nora to stop but knew she would risk being punished for speaking out of turn. There was no way she wanted to be on the receiving end of Sister Nora's anger.

Suddenly, Sister Nora dropped the crucifix, and it fell back against her chest. As if she had heard Katherine's thoughts, her eyes darted upwards and locked directly with Katherine's, piercing her with a malevolent stare. She smirked, as if she was taking pleasure causing terror in the young girl.

Katherine wanted to look away but found she couldn't. It was like she was frozen in place, having no choice but to succumb to the fear.

Sister Nora placed both hands on the table in front of her, leaning forward as if trying to get closer to Katherine. The smirk deepened.

Darkness began to close in on Katherine. The room was becoming blurry, and she felt dizzy.

Without warning, the sound of metal crashing against the wooden floors echoed throughout the room, breaking the spell between Katherine and Sister Nora. Everyone stopped, forks frozen in mid-air.

'I'm s-so sorry, Sister … I n-never intended to …' the young orphan who had dropped her fork stammered.

Katherine craned her neck to the side, trying to get a better view of the child, who was visibly trembling now. She sneered a little. She knew she should feel sorry for the girl, but she couldn't stop her unkind thoughts. *How pathetic! So anxious over a dropped fork!*

The girl was still pleading. 'I'm sorry,' she said. 'It won't ever happen again. I swear, Sister, please don't hurt ...' She stopped short, biting her bottom lip as though regretting her words.

Katherine raised her eyebrows in surprise.

The girls sitting next to the unfortunate orphan started to move away from her, as if eager to create as much distance as possible between them. This only motivated the girl to beg for forgiveness so fast that her words were lost in a string of garbled noise. Katherine was shocked to find she wanted to chuckle at the absurdity of it all.

'Christine! Come see me after lights out tonight,' Sister Nora barked at the girl, then slapped the palm of her hand against the table, causing the water glasses to vibrate, and everyone went right back to eating.

The young girl's face went white, as if every ounce of blood had suddenly been drained from her body.

Katherine couldn't understand how Sister Nora's few words could have that much of an effect on her. Bewildered, she stole a glance at Rose, hoping for an explanation, but Rose offered nothing in return. Instead, she brought her index finger up to her lips, indicating that Katherine was to remain silent, then bent her head over the table. Looking around the room, Katherine saw that every other girl had done the same. She assumed they were eager not to draw any unwanted attention to themselves.

The young girl began to cry silently, her whole body shuddering with the effort of remaining quiet, but no one came to her aid. A heavy air of fear pervaded the dining room. Katherine didn't need to look up again to know Sister Nora was still watching her. She could feel her eyes boring into the side of her face.

The next morning there was an empty spot at the table where the girl had sat the evening before. Everyone acted as if nothing had happened, as though she'd never been there in the first place.

IV

Katherine was baffled by everyone's willingness to keep up the pretence that Christine never existed within the walls of the convent. She needed to clear her head, so after her chores were done, she decided to go for a walk around the freezing-cold grounds. A gust of wind hit her face as soon as she stepped across the threshold, but considering the insanity that was penetrating the convent, she figured that some icy weather was nothing compared with what was happening inside.

She trudged along the gravel path, her nose growing red and her teeth chattering from the cold morning air. She wrapped her shawl tighter against her body as she approached the small graveyard that she'd seen from her bedroom window. Thinking she would bypass the resting place of the dead, she increased her pace but stopped when she noticed two small figures huddled together inside the graveyard. They were too far away for her to recognise them, but her curiosity got the better of her and, before she knew it, she was opening the gate and heading in their direction.

As she got closer to them, she noticed that their grimy faces were stained with tears, and they were gripping one another. She wasn't sure if they were trying to keep warm or finding solace in each other's company.

'What are you doing?' Katherine asked as she drew nearer. 'You're going to freeze to death just standing here, you know.'

Startled by Katherine's sudden appearance, both girls jumped away from each other, struggling to stay upright in the dense mud in which they were standing.

'What do you think you're doing, sneaking up on us?' one of them hissed at her. 'You nearly scared us half to death.'

Katherine's mouth fell open, surprised by this serious overreaction to her arrival. The girls looked a little older than her, around sixteen, she guessed. She recognised their faces from dinner the evening before.

'You're the new girl, Katherine, aren't you?' the other girl asked.

Katherine thought this girl was the more approachable of the two. Her mass of curly, auburn curls whipped around her face, and she struggled to keep the strands from getting in her eyes. She was wearing a worn grey frock with a neckline that was curling from age, allowing Katherine to see a scattering of bruises across her upper chest. The varying colours of yellow and purple showed that some were more recent than others.

'I'm Lauren, and this is Grace,' she said, gesturing to the other girl, who was still glaring at Katherine.

'What do you want?' Grace barked and folded her arms across her chest.

Clearly, this girl had no interest in being civil towards her. Katherine narrowed her eyes at Grace's gruff tone as she scrutinised her. Grace's gaunt face and sunken eyes did very little to help her appearance. With her pale complexion, she resembled a ghost. Her hair looked like it had been roughly shaven off; some patches were thicker than others, and some were so closely shaven that her scalp was red and raw in parts.

Deciding not to anger Grace any further by commenting on her odd appearance, Katherine addressed her previous question with an exaggerated eye-roll as if to say, *Isn't it obvious?* 'I was just out walking, and I saw you both. I wanted to see what you were doing, standing here in the graveyard.'

'We're saying goodbye to Aoife,' Lauren said. She bent down and placed a handful of thistles on the grave behind her.

Katherine stifled a laugh. 'You know those are weeds you're putting on the grave? They're not flowers.' She moved closer to the small headstone, ignoring Grace's perpetual glare. She read the name that was etched upon it – Aoife Crowley. The earth around it looked freshly dug; Aoife must have only passed recently.

Lauren blushed and gazed down at her feet. 'We don't have anything else to put on her grave,' she murmured, before looking back at Katherine. 'The thistles kind of look like flowers. At least, that's what Aoife always used to say.'

'What happened to her?' Katherine asked.

'What do you think happened to her?' Grace cried. 'It's the same thing that happens to everyone here after a while. It's *her*, she just—'

'Hush,' Lauren said as she placed her hand across Grace's mouth. 'Don't say any more.' She looked around in a panic. 'You know she can hear you. She can hear everything.'

The wind suddenly ceased as Lauren uttered those words. It was as if everything around them stood still, afraid of making even a decibel of noise.

'Who are you talking about?' Katherine asked. Her hands began shaking, whether from the cold or apprehension, she wasn't sure, but she clenched them into fists to try to stop the tremors.

Grace pushed Lauren's hand away from her face and rubbed her mouth in disgust, before spitting on the ground. 'Don't put your hand on my mouth!' she shouted. 'You know that she needs to know,' and she gestured in disdain at Katherine.

Lauren looked at Katherine with wide eyes. Her chin started to tremble as she struggled to stop the onslaught of tears that threatened to come. She glanced around again before shaking her head in defeat and beckoning for Grace to continue.

Grace nodded her head at her, welcoming the opportunity to continue her explanation. 'It's Sister Nora. After a while, everyone meets their demise at her hand. We don't know why, but even if we do everything right, nor draw any attention to ourselves, it doesn't matter. Everyone's fate is sealed. She submits us to horrendous abuse, sometimes for days at a time. It becomes so unbearable that sometimes you'd just wish it would all end. And you beg for God to make that happen, but it never does. God never answers our pleas. Only the lucky ones, like Aoife here, get to escape the hell we're living in.'

Grace rubbed her head and winced. Lauren reached out and rubbed her arm in sympathy, but Grace shrugged her off.

'Is that what happened to your head?' Katherine asked.

Grace folded her arms across her chest again and huffed. 'Well, I didn't do it to myself now, did I? Like I said, everyone gets the same treatment, so you'd best prepare yourself for what's to come. If you're lucky, you'll only have to endure it for a short time before you end up like Aoife.'

Grace took Lauren's arm and pulled her away, leaving Katherine alone in the graveyard to absorb what she had just been told. *Is no one safe here?* she wondered.

V

A few weeks later after dinner one night, the orphans walked in unison back to their dorm rooms as usual. The only sound was the rhythmic thudding of footsteps as each orphan walked in sync with each other. The line of girls grew shorter until only Katherine was left to return to her room. One of the nuns always followed the orphans to lock them in their rooms.

Rose had explained that as soon as the eleven o'clock bell rang, they were all expected to say a decade of the rosary before going to bed. Tonight, Katherine rushed to change into her nightdress and gingerly knelt at the side of her bed. The floorboards were hard and cold against her knees, but she tried not to focus on that too much as she swayed from side to side to try to alleviate some of the pain. She took out her rosary beads and had just managed to half-heartedly whisper her way through a verse of 'Hail Mary', when the wooden latch on her bedroom door swung open and hit the wall from the sheer force used.

Every girl's room had a hatch on the door. They had been created by Sister Nora herself so she could look in on the orphans. Katherine had heard the other nuns say that it was for their own safety, so they could 'check on the girls to make sure they were alright'. However, everyone knew it was due to Sister Nora's desire for complete control. Every one of the orphanage's processes was governed by control. The hatches let Sister Nora check that the orphans were following her commands, even in their isolated moments. Instead of feeling safe in the confines of their rooms where they should be able to rest from Sister Nora's gruelling schedule, their privacy was invaded. Even in their most private moments, she could easily single out those who were being lax in obeying her demands.

Luckily, by now Katherine was well used to the tyrannical nature of Sister Nora. She had been caught slacking in her prayers during her first few weeks in the convent and knew never to make the same fatal mistake again. Remembering that night made Katherine suddenly feel cold. She had been so preoccupied with her own thoughts that night, trying to make sense of why everyone was always so on edge, that she hadn't heard the bell ring. When Sister Nora came around for her usual inspections, Katherine hadn't been kneeling at the side of her bed as she should have been. In an instant, she learnt the answer to the question that had been dominating her mind – was no one safe here? Sister Nora, staring through the hatch with a face like thunder, declared that she was to follow her to her office at once, and she unlocked the bedroom door.

Katherine shuffled along the dark, ominous hallway behind Sister Nora towards her private office. She couldn't remember the last time she had been in such close proximity to the head nun, other than her very first day at the orphanage. Sister Nora preferred to keep a watch over the orphans from a distance rather than engaging directly with them, so the fact that Katherine was on her own with this woman terrified her to her very core. Sister Nora swung open her office door and stood aside for Katherine to enter. It took a few moments for Katherine's feet to move again, so Sister Nora pushed her roughly over the threshold, causing her to stumble into the room.

Katherine shivered as she stood in front of the wooden desk in the middle of the room. Sister Nora had given her no chance to change out of her nightdress, and the icy-cold night air made her bones rattle. The nun sat down behind the desk and relaxed back into her chair, giving the impression that she was completely at ease. She tapped her fingers one by one on the wooden desk and a chilling smile appeared on her face as she stared at Katherine.

Finally, she broke the silence. 'You forget your place, girl!' she barked. 'You are here because you are utterly alone in this world. You are here because you have *no one*. And yet, even though you're barely in the door, you feel as if you can disobey my rules. Why is that?'

Sister Nora paused and sprang up from her seat. 'You think you're better than the rest of the orphans, don't you, Katherine? This cannot go unpunished.' She let out an exaggerated breath, shook her head and walked towards an aged brown cabinet at the side of the room. She opened its heavy doors and pulled out a thin riding crop.

Katherine swallowed. Her mouth had gone dry.

Sister Nora continued. 'My rules will always be followed here because, within these walls, I am the only power, the only God you need to know.' She swished the crop back and forth as she circled Katherine. 'Raise your nightdress above your knees and repeat after me, I am alone.'

'I am alo—' Katherine's breath hitched as she felt the sharp lash of the crop hit the back of her knees. The sudden shock of the pain made it impossible for her to speak.

'Again!' Sister Nora shouted as she sliced the crop through the air, her voice becoming shrill as she shouted at her.

'I am a-alone,' Katherine stammered through gritted teeth.

'I have no one,' Sister Nora snarled while hitting her again.

The stinging on the back of her legs made it difficult to concentrate on repeating the words back to her verbatim. Tears threatened, but Katherine fought hard to hold them back. She wouldn't give Sister Nora the satisfaction of showing her pain or that her words and actions were upsetting her. She had to see this ordeal through until Sister Nora had had enough of inflicting her abuse.

'I have no one.' *Crack*. 'I am alone.' *Crack*.

The sound of the crop cracking against her skin oddly gave Katherine something to focus on rather than the physical pain. She had managed to disassociate herself from the agony ripping through her body and focus her mind on counting each time the crop whipped the back of her knees.

She wasn't sure how much time passed before Sister Nora finally threw the crop onto her desk. She was gasping for air from the exertion of wielding the crop with such pressure against Katherine's skin.

Katherine forced herself to glance up at Sister Nora, whose face was flushed with anger. A vein bulged from the side of her neck, indicating that the nun was still furious with her. Clearly, carrying out Katherine's punishment had done little to minimise her aggravation.

Despite the sheer amount of pain coursing through her body, Katherine surprised herself by returning the nun's cold stare, thinking, *You want to break me ... to wear me down like all the other orphans ... to see me cry and beg. But I'm not like the other pathetic urchins in this place. I refuse to let you win!* And she glared at her in defiance.

Sister Nora's eyes narrowed, and she recommenced whipping Katherine but with increased strength, trying to make her crumble. When she stopped a short while later, she leaned down and whispered into Katherine's right ear, her husky breath making the hair on the back of Katherine's neck stand up.

'I told you before, none of our children ever truly leave us. You would do best to remember that.'

She straightened her back and returned to her desk. 'You are nothing in this world, Katherine,' she declared while toying with the chain on her neck. 'Let this be your first and final warning. You will obey my word.' And she dismissed Katherine with a flick of her hand.

Katherine hobbled her way back to her room, closing the door with a gentle push behind her. Finally, she let the tears pour out as she tentatively rubbed the backs of her knees. The skin was swollen and raw. It would be at least a couple of days before she would be able to walk without wincing from the pain. She turned and slammed her hands against the wall in anger. Every step she took until then would be a constant reminder of the wrath of Sister Nora, a reminder that she was always watching and waiting for one of the girls to make a mistake so she could abuse them in some way for her own sick entertainment. Katherine threw herself on to her bed and sobbed uncontrollably into her arms. What was to happen to her here?

As she lay in bed later that night, her mind replayed the heinous event that had occurred. Her active mind and the pain from her wounded skin were preventing her from sleeping. It must have been close to around three in the morning, she guessed, when she felt a low vibration which disrupted her tired train of thought. She couldn't work out what was causing it, but it seemed to be coming from right underneath her. Gingerly, she crept towards the door, but the vibration lessened. Next, she tried lying flat on the ground and pressing her palms against the floorboards. There it was! She could feel it perfectly from that angle. She frowned, but then it dawned on her.

The chapel was located under her room, which meant the vibration could have only been coming from somebody playing the organ. But who, at this early hour, and why? She crawled back into bed, her mind buzzing with this new information. Eventually, thanks to the constant hum from below, Katherine managed to drift off to sleep. She slept heavily, her dreams filled with images of a shining crucifix and a lonely chapel.

VI

The following morning, after yet another questionable meal of murky-looking porridge, the orphans were labouring in the gardens. Katherine's hands smarted from the scratchy shrubs she was tending. She leaned back on her heels and turned to Rose, who was weeding the section next to her. 'Rose, I think someone was playing the organ in the chapel in the early hours. There was this strange vibration coming from below my room.'

The blood drained from Rose's face. Her hand shook and the weeds she'd been clutching tumbled to the ground. 'Shhh, don't say anything else; you're going to get us both in trouble,' she whispered and scrambled to pick up the fallen weeds.

'Why would we get in trouble for talking?' Katherine asked, 'We're not doing anything wrong.'

Rose glanced at the other girls before lowering her voice further and saying, 'I don't know what you want me to say, Katherine. Strange things happen here; sometimes they just can't be explained. It's safer for you … and everyone … if you stop trying to find answers.'

Katherine thought for a moment, but fear or no fear, she needed answers. She pressed Rose again. 'Just tell me the truth, and I won't ever bring it up again. I need to know what is going on here.'

Rose looked at her and shook her head in exasperation.

Katherine felt a twinge of guilt for making the other girl uncomfortable, but thought she saw a glimmer of understanding in Rose's eyes. Perhaps she was beginning to win the young girl over. She bent over her patch of garden again, hoping to look busy and to placate Rose. She spoke from the side of her mouth so no one would realise they were talking. 'Surely, you must have felt it too,' Katherine pleaded. 'I mean, your room is right next to mine.'

Rose shook her head in denial. 'The only thing I hear at night is Emma snoring from across the room!'

Katherine scoffed in frustration. Rose really wasn't giving in easily. Through gritted teeth she said, 'Look, Rose, enough is enough. I don't believe you. Strange things are happening here, but there must be a logical explanation. Everything seems to point to Sister Nora. And you wouldn't be so scared if you didn't have the answers. Please, just be honest with me. We both have to live here. I need to know what's happening too.'

Rose looked at Katherine, eyes wide with fear. Her shoulders slumped, and she gestured for Katherine to continue with her task. 'Okay, I'll tell you what I know, but at least make it look like you're working.' Rose sighed and pushed a strand of hair out of her eyes before continuing.

'There was a girl here a few months ago,' Rose said. 'I think they called her Aislinn or something, and she heard things in the night too that no one else ever did. She felt like she was going crazy. She went to Sister Nora after the six o'clock service one evening, even though the girls warned her against it …' Rose paused and looked around, making sure they still weren't drawing any unwanted attention.

'Why?' Katherine asked.

'You know very well what happens when you're alone with Sister Nora in her office. You're not the only one walking around with healing wounds.' Rose took a deep, steadying breath before she went on.

'Nobody saw Aislinn again after her meeting with Sister Nora. All her things were gone from her room the next day. It's like she never existed here. None of the other nuns would even speak of her. That's why you're the only one who has a spare bed in your room. That's where Aislinn slept.'

Katherine spent the next few days trying to find out more from the other girls, but they remained tight-lipped. Whenever she tried to approach the subject, their eyes would flash with fear, and they would stutter excuses about needing to be somewhere else. They began to either avoid her or to look at her as if she was going mad. They would whisper amongst themselves, glancing over at Katherine, making her feel like an outsider. It appeared that Sister Nora's wrath had successfully bought their silence, leaving the nun full reign to continue operating under a shroud of mystery.

Yet Katherine didn't give up on her mission to find answers. One morning, lost in thought about who else in the convent she might ask, the cathedral bells rang to signify midday. She hadn't even noticed the morning slipping away from her. As she looked up from her work and wiped away the sweat dripping from her brow, she caught a glimpse of Father Michael blessing a local woman by the chapel doors. He was scheduled to carry out confessions throughout the course of the day.

He caught Katherine staring at him and offered a warm yet fleeting smile and walked back into the chapel. His friendly smile gave Katherine a little sliver of hope. Perhaps, he might be able to help her.

Katherine had been known in her hometown as cunning – 'too wise for her age' was what they used to say about her. She always knew how to get what she wanted, and she knew well enough that as Father Michael was a well-established clergyman, he was bound to silence by his vows. Whatever she would say to him would remain confidential.

She thought about her mother's words many years ago as she was preparing for her first confession. 'What is said between a priest and a parishioner during confession is sacred. Anything you tell him is private. It's between you and God; the priest is just the middleman. He has taken a vow of secrecy that cannot be broken.'

A vow of secrecy is very useful in this case, she thought. And so she decided that after lunch, she would go to confession to speak with Father Michael.

VII

When she walked into the cold and draughty chapel that afternoon, Father Michael was already concealed within the confines of the confessional box. Katherine sighed with relief as his concealment bought her a few more moments of anonymity. Her stomach knotted in anxiety. Would he recognise her voice as soon as she spoke? She couldn't think about that possibility now. The sheer desire for answers heavily outweighed any thought of not going through with her plan.

She pulled back the heavy red velvet curtain and stepped inside the narrow space. Her heart thumping in her chest, she knelt on the pew and took a deep breath to steady herself. The curtain was so thick that as soon as she pulled it shut behind her, she was encased in complete darkness. The strong smell of frankincense threatened to overpower her senses but helped to calm her nerves a little. There was an odd comfort to the smell. It reminded her of the early weekday mornings when her mother had insisted upon dragging her out of bed at an ungodly hour to hear the six am service being said before the day had even begun. She let out a huff of breath that she didn't realise she'd been holding, shaking her head to clear the memories that were threatening to come to the surface.

Everything was silent in the confessional for a few moments, and she wondered if Father Michael had perhaps not heard her enter. She shuffled awkwardly on the seat to let him know she was there, and the wooden shutter snapped open, causing a sharp noise to echo through the box. She couldn't make out his face clearly but knew it was Father Michael from the outline of his shadow on the wooden wall behind him.

She gulped. She had been so confident with her plan earlier in the day, but now she wasn't so sure. She reminded herself why she was there and, adopting the role of a young girl asking for absolution, she began. 'Bless me, Father, for I have sinned. In the eyes of others, I have been asking blasphemous questions.' Katherine rolled her eyes. She tried to make her voice sound regretful. She had to tread with caution here in case Father Michael completely shut down and refused to speak with her.

'And have you, my child? Have you been asking such questions?' Father Michael asked.

'No. I don't believe I have. I've only been asking about why someone appears to be playing the chapel organ every night around 3 am.'

Father Michael gasped. His shadow moved on the wall in a jerky fashion. 'My child. This really isn't the place to speak of such things,' he said, anxiety pitching his voice high. 'I strongly urge you to—'

'I know that you see what happens here,' Katherine interrupted. 'The missing orphans – I saw you bless yourself from my window last week when the caretaker disposed of a body during the rainy spell. The remaining children are too afraid to even speak in case they draw attention to themselves. Nobody wants to risk it in case something happens to them. Oh! And let's not forget Sister Nora's absurd fascination with the crucifix she wears. You must have seen her too – pulling and tugging at the chain on her neck like a woman possessed. And that odd darkness in her eyes. You have the answers. I know you do. I am stuck in this orphanage with nowhere to go. The very least you can do is let me know what darkness lies within these walls.'

Father Michael began muttering and blessing himself with a string of rosary beads. He let out a deep sigh. 'Like I said, this isn't the place for this … but … I will give you what you seek,' he whispered. 'After the nine o'clock service tonight, meet me in my chambers. It should be safe to talk there. In the meantime, my child, for your sake, it would be best to not utter a word of this to anyone. Try to remain as discreet as you can.'

Katherine didn't respond to Father Michael, but out of habit, she blessed herself before exiting the confessional box. At last, he'd explain everything to her. For now, she had to be patient.

VIII

The remainder of the dull winter's day dragged achingly slowly. Every tick of the clock reminded Katherine that she was growing closer to learning what wickedness lay within the walls of the orphanage. She couldn't concentrate on the monotonous drawl of the nine o'clock sermon. The priest's words had become a dull noise in the back of her head as she examined every possible scenario that Father Michael might explain. If it wasn't for the other girls sitting in her pew, she wouldn't have even known whether it was time for her to sit or stand.

A knot had formed in the depths of her stomach. She caught Rose's eye from across the chapel. Rose raised her brows as if to ask if she was alright, but Katherine just smiled back and clasped her hands together, pretending to focus back on her prayers. Her little charade seemed to fool Rose, who turned her head to face the altar again. Katherine made a mental note to calm down. She couldn't risk drawing any unwanted attention to herself. The night had to go according to plan; not one detail could be out of place.

After almost an eternity, the mass was finally over, and the rest of the orphans made their way to do their nightly chores.

They all spilled out of the main double doors, eager to get started on their allocated jobs so they could go to bed. While the rest of them pushed past each other to make their way down the hall, Katherine broke off from the crowd and darted in the opposite direction.

Katherine made her way down the damp, stone corridor towards Father Michael's chambers. She was concerned that Sister Nora would notice she wasn't doing her chores, but her need for answers gave her the strength to carry on. Cautiously, she looked around to make sure no one had followed her. She raised her fist, hesitating for a moment, and knocked on the heavy wooden door of Father Michael's room.

His response was barely audible, but she thought she heard a faint 'Enter' in reply.

She pushed open the door and tiptoed across the creaky threshold. The room was in total darkness. The only glimmer of light came from a small candle burning in a holder on a desk pushed back against the wall. Father Michael had his back to her, consumed with the task of writing in a worn leather-bound book. He placed the dip pen back in the pot of black ink, but still didn't turn to face her. Instead, he pulled over a rickety chair and placed it by the side of the desk, glancing over his shoulder, gesturing for her to take a seat.

'What are you writing?' she asked, craning her neck to read over his shoulder.

Instead of answering her, Father Michael slammed the book shut, bound it with a fraying leather strap and placed it in a narrow cupboard underneath the desk. He made a show of locking it with a bronze key that he pulled from his pocket. From his clenched jaw, Katherine surmised that he hadn't liked her questioning him about his writing. Before he closed the cupboard door, Katherine had seen at least another ten books of the same design. Were they journals? Would their contents tell her what she needed to know? She decided not to push the issue further for now. She would have to figure out a way to see the contents of the books at a later stage.

A heavy silence hung in the air. She was getting sick of all these awkward moments. Studying Father Michael's face, she assumed he was battling with some deep-rooted internal conflict. His nervousness was palpable, and his mouth kept opening and closing, as though he wanted to speak but was incapable of uttering a word. She knew what she was asking him to do was a difficult task. He was probably breaking a handful of the orphanage's rules by even meeting with her, let alone telling her its secrets.

She rolled her neck in frustration. Time was passing, and she had to be back in line with the other girls by bedtime. Her eyes wandered to a small, faded photograph hanging on the back of the door. She squinted and recognised the two figures in at as Father Michael and Sister Nora. They were both smiling, like two children at the peak of happiness. They both looked much younger.

'You knew her. I mean, before she was like this. Didn't you?' Katherine asked, barely above a whisper.

Father Michael's Adam's apple bobbed in his pale throat, giving Katherine all the confirmation she needed.

The priest's eyes darted to the photograph and he let out a deep sigh. 'She was a great friend of mine,' he said with a brief smile. 'A true companion. The type of companion that one can only dream of having in life, but all that changed as her obsession with the crucifix grew ...'

'What is so special about the crucifix?' Katherine blurted out. 'It looks different from the other ones I've seen Sister Sarah and Sister Eunice wearing, but surely they are all the same, aren't they?'

Father Michael rested both of his palms on the desk before reaching underneath it and pulling out a bottle of brandy. Judging by how little was left in the bottle, Katherine guessed that he must have started drinking it long before she entered the room. *Maybe he needed it for courage,* she thought. He leaned in closer, the pungent smell of brandy wafting on his breath as he spoke.

'The crucifix that Sister Nora wears is known to be biblical in its origin. Those worn by the rest of the sisterhood are generic, more symbolic, if you will. They all come from the little sacristy shop next to the cathedral in town. In essence, there's nothing noteworthy about them, but it ensures uniformity. I am sure that you are familiar with the story of how Judas betrayed Jesus, are you not?'

Katherine gave a meek nod of her head, wondering where Father Michael was going with his story and what it had to do with Sister Nora's ostentatious crucifix.

Father Michael stretched his fingers, his bones cracking as he moved. 'No one fully knows why Judas chose to betray him, other than the fact he was given thirty pieces of silver from the temple priest for his actions,' he said frankly. 'However, that's not all he received. It isn't noted in the scriptures because the object Judas received was stolen from his own dead body before the authorities could even make a note of it. The missing object, I'm sure you can probably guess, is the very same crucifix which hangs from the neck of Sister Nora.'

Father Michael stopped for a moment and looked at Katherine over the top of his reading glasses, ensuring that she was fully absorbing what he was saying.

'It has been said that a wandering shepherd came across the body of Judas while he was on his way to tend to his lowly flock. At first, he was horrified by the sight in front of him, as most would be. The harsh, isolated place in which he was found and the grotesque expression of pain that was fixed on Judas' face because his soul was destined to descend into hell was quite a scene to behold. While taking everything in, the shepherd noticed something shining on the ground beneath the body. Dotted around in multiple places lay the thirty pieces of silver, as if Judas had cast them to the ground in a mad fury before deciding to end his own life.

'Overcome by sheer greed, the poor shepherd quickly gathered the coins before anyone else could see what he was doing. When he stood up, he felt something hit the back of his head. Startled, he quickly turned around, dropping some of the coins in shock, and observed a gold crucifix dangling from Judas' rigid hand. The minute his eyes locked with the gold crucifix, something in him changed.

'Some say he heard voices, that the crucifix began whispering to him about the power and greatness he could possess. The coins no longer mattered to him, and he completely forgot about the existence of his flock. He snatched the crucifix from Judas' hand and took off across the hills, never to be seen again. They say that he was lost to the Devil forever.'

Katherine held her hands up to stop Father Michael from speaking. 'I'm not sure I understand you, Father,' she said, shaking her head in confusion. None of it made any sense to her. 'How can someone be lost to the Devil by simply taking a crucifix? It's just an object.'

Father Michael glanced at Katherine as he leaned on the desk before emphasising his next point. 'The Gospel says that as soon as Judas received the piece of bread that Jesus offered him during the Last Supper, Satan entered him. However, that's not necessarily true.' He rubbed his temples.

'For, you see, Satan had already entered Judas the moment he decided to betray those close to him. The very moment his hand touched the crucifix, Satan used it as a gateway to have

Judas do his bidding. The crucifix had become tainted by sin, taking control of the dark side that was festering within Judas.' He rubbed the spot between his eyebrows vigorously.

'You see, child, everyone has some level of darkness within them; it's ultimately what makes us human. God and the Devil have coexisted within everyone since the beginning of time. What separates us, is which power we succumb to. Have you ever wondered why some people are capable of committing monstrous, completely unholy acts and yet others seem incapable of hurting even the smallest of insects?'

He went on without giving her a chance to answer.

'It's because they give in to the evil residing within them. Over the years, there has been a string of ghastly events with people ending up dead. In each case, the same crucifix has been sighted on the neck of somebody connected with the dead person. Those who wear it have no control over their actions once the crucifix touches their neck. After a while, the people completely change in character. They become darker, their actions sadistic and their thoughts deeply sinister. The crucifix has been involved in so much death and destruction over the centuries that it's become a sort of gateway for evil. It calls out to the next viable human soul like a siren, providing the unknowing soul with a glimpse of the immense power they can possess. Once it touches human skin, it's as if people are finally able to succumb to the will of the Devil and complete whatever atrocious actions he desires. It knows what lies deep within the person's soul, what they've managed to keep at bay for years, and it feeds off it, growing more malevolent after each situation.'

Katherine was sitting bolt upright as she listened to his tale. This time, she was the one who was lost for words.

'Whoever wears that crucifix is destined to complete grave atrocities, and every time another death occurs, the evil grows stronger. That's why so many bad things have happened here,' he finally admitted.

'How did the crucifix even end up in this orphanage if it dates back to biblical times?' Katherine asked.

'Like many antiquities, so to speak, it has been shipped around the world over time and passed down through generations. It just so happens that the previous Reverend Mother, Sister Bernadette, inherited the crucifix from her own sister, following her death.'

'What happened to Sister Bernadette?' Katherine asked with a shaky breath, already dreading the answer.

Father Michael hesitated. He had anticipated that Katherine would ask this very question, but it still didn't prepare him for the mental turmoil of reliving what had happened to the previous Reverend Mother. It was as if the question itself had brought him back to that time, and he was witnessing the horror of it all over again.

'Towards the end of Sister Bernadette's reign in the orphanage, I was concerned for her safety. Sister Nora's fascination with Bernadette's crucifix was beginning to surpass insurmountable levels. It was all she could speak of. It was consuming her.

'There were times when I watched her secretly, and it was as if she was in a hypnotic trance. She would stare at Sister Bernadette and stroke her own neck, as if imagining the crucifix resting there. At that point, it wasn't even in her possession.

'It wasn't too long before there was a series of tragedies in the orphanage. Bernadette kept showing up with injuries that she passed off as being caused by accidents, you know, falling down the stairs and things like that. She seemed quite skittish of everyone too, but there was no concrete explanation as to what had caused the sudden change in her character. She didn't want to speak of it and so, I never pushed her. I thought she wasn't comfortable disclosing any information to me.' The orphans were terrified too, but when I questioned them they remained silent. I think they knew who was responsible for the "accidents".'

He stopped to gulp more brandy before he continued. 'Sister Nora was becoming less like the friend I had grown fond of. There was a shocking darkness about her. Even her eyes seemed to change; they used to hold such warmth and optimism, but any light that had once been present was long gone. At the time, I couldn't explain it, but knowing what I do now, I believe the crucifix was already speaking to her immoral side, controlling her and pulling her towards it. That darkness was impossible to break through, despite my sincerest efforts. After a while I realised, for the sake of my own life, I needed to keep a safe distance from her. I was afraid she would do the same things to me that she had done to those poor students. I know what you're thinking. It was weak of me to distance myself, but you've seen what she can do. You've experienced the pain she can cause, and no one wants to be on the receiving end of that.

'Some of the orphans had begun to whisper about strange noises coming from the chapel late at night. Some said they could even feel vibrations coming from the floorboards. There was one girl whose room was directly above the chapel. I don't think she had been here very long, but she claimed that someone was playing the organ in the wee hours.'

Father Michael fidgeted in his seat. 'Of course, at the time, there was no proof, and we thought the children were just making up stories as a ... coping mechanism, if you like. The stories were just so odd. I would've never believed them myself, were it not for one grim night – the night where I saw first-hand the true unmitigated power that the crucifix is capable of.'

Father Michael gazed off into the distance, his brow furrowed as he became haunted by the memories that had been stirred up. He thought he had buried them deep within himself.

'I was working late in my chambers one night, and at about three in the morning, I felt the vibration myself. It was so strong it seemed to exude from the floorboards and up the walls. It continued for a few moments and then stopped. At first, I thought it must have come from the old pipes in the building. Old pipes are notorious for rattling before they settle. But then it happened again. It was bizarre. I wondered if it was one of the new girls playing a trick, so I rushed to the chapel to try to catch the culprit in the act. Instead, what I found shook me to the very core. It was truly horrific. I'll never be able to forget it. It made me question my faith.'

He rubbed his eyes as though trying to erase the image. 'Sister Nora was standing over the lifeless body of Sister Bernadette, who was lying crumpled in a heap on the altar steps. I could tell she was gone the moment I looked at her. There was so much blood … so much. The glow from the candelabras was creating a dull light around them. I thought perhaps she hadn't noticed me standing in the darkness because she didn't turn around to face me. But thinking back now, her whole demeanour showed she was too strongly connected to the crucifix at that point to even care about being caught.'

He raised his index finger just as Katherine opened her mouth to interrupt him. 'Let me finish. Nora had fortified her connection to the Devil by committing the most heinous sin imaginable. She wanted the crucifix so badly that she was willing to kill for it. She threw away her vows and everything holy that she believed in.'

He paused and shifted in his seat. 'She was clutching a blood-splattered candlestick so tightly, her knuckles were white. I was wondering what I should do when she suddenly hit Sister Bernadette across the side of her head, even though she was already dead. The sound of it paralysed me.' He shook his head, and a tear escaped the corner of one eye.

'The sheer force she was exerting forced droplets of sweat from her forehead to fall onto Sister Bernadette's face, making it look like she was crying. It was the most horrific thing I've ever had to bear witness to.'

He swallowed the lump that was beginning to form in his throat. 'When she stopped, she leaned down right into Sister Bernadette's face. By now, I could clearly see her face … and she was smiling! She snatched the crucifix from Sister Bernadette's neck and tossed the candlestick to the side, causing a clattering noise to echo throughout the empty chapel. I watched her stand up and place the crucifix around her own neck. The few candles that had remained alight throughout this horrible act suddenly died, but there was no gust of air in the chapel that could explain it. It was clear to me that God's presence was no longer in the chapel.'

Father Michael made eye contact with Katherine. 'Sister Nora looked directly at me then and said without any emotion, "I require some assistance, Father Michael. It seems that Sister Bernadette has had a most unfortunate accident".'

IX

Katherine jumped up, almost knocking her chair over in the process, and had to steady herself by placing her arm on the nearby wall. 'You helped her cover it up!' she said, her voice rising in anger. 'You've known for years what she is capable of, what the crucifix has made her do, and you've helped her every step along the way. How can you, as a "man of God", answer to that? You're meant to protect us! Have you no shame?'

'I accepted my fate long ago.' Father Michael's speech was slurred. He drained the last drop of brandy that was left in the bottle. 'I know that when the judgement day finally comes, I will be made to answer for my sins. I have no answer that you will ever find acceptable for what I have done. I think, looking back on it now, I just wanted to protect a friend but, as the years went by, I must admit, I was too afraid of the repercussions if I didn't help her and too ashamed to admit it.'

Katherine shook her head in disgust. 'How many deaths have you let slide because of your fear?' she hissed.

Father Michael slumped down in his chair and put his head in his hands and sobbed. Katherine didn't have any words of comfort to offer him. She was reeling from what she had heard, made worse by the fact that the man she had thought she could trust was Sister Nora's right-hand man in all the atrocities she had committed. Katherine didn't have the patience for his pitiful guilt. It was too late for that. If he had any remorse for his actions, he would have tried to do better, to help the girls in the orphanage.

'I am so sorry,' Father Michael whispered through his sobbing. 'She has eyes on you all the time, and there is nothing I can do to protect you …'

Katherine's blood ran cold at his admission. She now had confirmation that Sister Nora was indeed watching her from the shadows. She wasn't sure how to process that. It had been easier to pretend she could somehow exempt herself from the horrors of the place – that the violence she was subjected to was simply a punishment for not following orders.

Father Michael kept repeating how sorry he was, but Katherine had nothing to say to him in return. Instead, aware how much time had passed, she stormed out of the chapel and made it back in time to join the other girls on their way to their dorms.

When Sister Nora had finished her rounds that night, Katherine went straight to bed. Her heart was still racing at the recent revelations. Never in her wildest dreams had she imagined this would be her reality.

She didn't believe in the existence of the Devil. She always thought it was made up to get children to behave, but now she knew evil truly existed and it was operating within the convent's walls. She thought about the notebooks that the priest had tried to conceal from her. She guessed they would reveal a lot more to her than he had. She still had so many unanswered questions. Why was Sister Nora singling her out to be watched? It wouldn't be easy to find out or get hold of the key to retrieve Father Michael's journals. She would have to devise a plan.

X

Katherine spent the next few days mulling over the different options for obtaining the key from Father Michael without him knowing. Images of the exact moment she gained access to the cupboard ran in a loop through her head. She could see the outcome: the dual victory of pulling off the key heist and gaining all the answers to her questions. This vision made the blood pump through her veins.

She needed to know exactly what Sister Nora had planned for her. Katherine refused to believe it was too late for her to escape the nun's attention, as Father Michael did. She wasn't like the other girls. She couldn't live each day in anticipation of pain, hoping she might succumb to her injuries one day and escape this hellhole by dying. Her mother had always told her that she was a deceptive, resourceful child, so she figured now would be the perfect time to live up that reputation. It was time to use those traits to her advantage – to fight for her life.

The following week, when Sister Eunice was assigning all the orphans their chores for the week, she volunteered to clean the chapel.

'I'll do it, Sister,' she sang while raising her hand with a false level of enthusiasm.

All the girls hated this task and considered it akin to punishment. With every inch of the place right down to the pews and chalices needing to be meticulously polished and shined with beeswax, it was a time-consuming task. It wasn't unheard of for some of the girls' hand joints to lock from the repetitive task. It was usually reserved for those who had angered Sister Nora throughout the previous week, but not enough to warrant her usual abuse. She used it to torment them, ordering Sister Eunice to assign the role to whatever girl she had on her list.

'Why would you want to do that, Katherine?' Sister Eunice asked without even looking up.

She was a plump woman around thirty years old, with a round, bulging face and beady eyes. She was naturally suspicious about everything. Katherine had heard that she suffered from gout and couldn't stand for longer than a few minutes at a time. Katherine thought she was utterly useless, but she intended using the nun's weakness for her own benefit.

'The sooner you have someone to clean the chapel, the sooner you can cross it off your list and retire to your chambers. That is what you want, isn't it?'

'You, child,' the nun said with a sneer, 'would do best to keep your mouth shut. However, you can clean the chapel. I expect every surface to shine by the time you're finished. Off you go, everyone!' she screamed as she hobbled towards her dormitory.

Katherine cared little for the wellbeing of Sister Eunice's legs. She only wanted access to the chapel for one reason. Part of cleaning the chapel included cleaning the office, which is where Father Michael would leave his overgarments before beginning his sermon. It was the perfect chore for her to carry out her plan. Since she was excused from attending mass while she cleaned, she would have the perfect opportunity to slip the key out of his overcoat and return it before he even had a chance to notice that it was missing. Slipping items from people's pockets was one of her specialties, but she had never returned anything that she had taken before, so this part would be entirely new to her. *How hard can it be?* she thought.

After breakfast had finished on Tuesday morning, she went over to Father Michael's office to execute the first step in her plan. She greeted him with a brief 'Good morning, Father', as she entered, careful not to appear too excited in case he should become suspicious. She made her way over to the basin of holy water and blessed herself; she would need every bit of help from God today. Thankfully, Father Michael paid little attention to her as he was busy pouring over the Bible in preparation for his sermon.

Katherine started to dust the paintings at the far side of the room. She had to play her part in carrying out her chores, at least for a few minutes until Father Michael had left the room. She kept a discreet eye on him as she worked.

A few minutes later, he glanced over the top of his reading glasses at the antique clock on the wall and snapped the Bible closed, then disappeared inside the small room at the back of the office that he used for changing into his robes.

He emerged dressed in his priestly attire. 'Nearly lost track of time,' he said as he shuffled past. He gave her a quick nod, brushed off an invisible wrinkle on his robe and strode towards the chapel.

If it had been any other day, and if she didn't know his true nature, Katherine would have found his awkwardness quite humorous. She knew he was avoiding her, most likely afraid that she might tell someone his secret. Her opinion of him had changed drastically since his revelation. He disgusted her. Even looking at him made her curl her lip. But her new opinion of him made the execution of her plan so much easier. She didn't feel bad for stealing from a priest. In fact, she considered it a form of karmic retribution for the atrocities that he had helped cover up.

As soon as she heard the opening hymn begin to play, Katherine wasted no time. She dropped the duster on the floor and ran into the room where he had dressed only a few minutes prior. She thrust her hand into the right-hand pocket of his coarse coat and felt the key right away. She pulled it from the garment and looked down at the key in her palm. She'd done it. Now, all her nerves were gone, and she chuckled.

That was easy, she thought, but then realised she couldn't get ahead of herself. The hard part was yet to come. She only had approximately forty minutes to pull this off and she couldn't risk being caught. She strode over to the office door and eased it open, being careful not to allow the door to bang behind her. She didn't want Father Michael to hear it in the middle of his sermon.

She tiptoed down the steep steps outside, looking around her as she did to make sure there was no one around. Her gaze fell on a large rock that was part of the border of a flowerbed. She wedged the muddy rock at the corner of the doorframe to stop it from slamming and sprinted over to the main building towards Father Michael's own private chambers. The sound of the congregation chanting their prayers was ringing in her ears as she ran towards her destination.

'… as we forgive those who trespass against us; and lead us not into temptation but deliver us from evil …'

XI

The hallway was silent as Katherine, now out of breath, reached the door to Father Michael's chambers. The door was old and heavy. She had to use her shoulder to push it open a fraction, then squeezed her way in. As soon as she was safe inside, she shut the door and rested her back against it. She needed a moment to prepare herself for what she was about to find. She moved over to the cabinet beneath the desk and forced her shaking hand to remain still enough to insert the key.

Katherine smiled when she heard the faint click of the lock opening. Leaving the key in the cabinet door, she leaned back on her haunches and pulled both doors open. A gust of dust hit her in the face, and she stifled the resulting cough with her hand. There had to be at least ten identical notebooks inside. She wondered where to start, but figured the dustiest would be the oldest and, as such, would provide the information she needed.

She hauled the first book from the cabinet and placed it on Father Michael's chair, which she used as a makeshift table. Using the sleeve of her dress to wipe away the dust, she opened it to the first page. The text was so faded and yellow with age it was difficult to read. Katherine lit the small candle sitting on Father Michael's desk and brought it right up next to the book, which helped a little, but she could only make out a few distinct words. And what she could decipher shocked her.

'Bludgeoned. Tortured … severed tongue.' Pages and pages of descriptions of brutal acts against the orphanage's occupants, all documented with precision, as if he had simply been making one of his daily mundane reports.

Her blood ran cold, and her breathing became shallow. She knew that Father Michael had been covering for Sister Nora, but she hadn't considered the extent of the nun's actions. She had been abusing both the orphans and staff alike for as long as she had been working in the orphanage. Such inexplicable cruelty from one woman, due to the maleficent powers attached to the ancient crucifix that owned her. And with the help of one man who hid the truth as she continued her sadistic practices.

She was so consumed by her own terrified thoughts that she hadn't even noticed that her short breathing had extinguished the candle she was holding. With shaking and sweating hands, she managed to relight the candle and placed the book to one side, starting a little pile next to her. She apprehensively grabbed the next book and braced herself with half-squinted eyes for what was going to be contained within its stiff spine.

Feeling sick with apprehension at what else she would discover, she grabbed another book. The worn spine opened automatically to the middle page. The text was handwritten in black ink and was set out like a type of ledger. There were pages full of names and ages of girls with a corresponding year and date underlined next to each one. At first, she couldn't make sense of it, but then she found a name with the current year, and it suddenly dawned on her.

'Siobhan Madigan, September 2nd, 1865.'

The bile rose in her throat, and she felt like she was going to throw up. Katherine had first come to the orphanage on the afternoon of September 2nd, and that was when she had witnessed the caretaker moving a dead body in a wheelbarrow.

She remembered hearing some of the girls whispering that night, saying something bad must have happened to a girl called Siobhan as she hadn't come back to the dormitory since Sister Nora had called her into her office. Katherine tried to shake off a feeling of dread as she scrolled down through the rest of the names on the page. Her finger stopped below another familiar name – 'Aoife Crowley'. Her stomach lurched, and her hand flew to her mouth. She rushed to the nearby waste basket and gagged.

The name of Aoife Crowley stuck out to her like a shining beacon for several reasons. Not only was this the name attached to the very recent headstone in the graveyard where she had encountered Grace and Lauren a few weeks earlier, but there was a photograph of Aoife hanging in the main hallway, a fake smile that didn't reach her eyes plastered upon her ghostly pale face.

Katherine's body felt weak. Her legs threatened to crumple beneath her. The ledger of names was the names of all of Sister Nora's victims throughout the years. Father Michael had kept a record of every single one. She didn't know whether it was because of guilt or the fact that he may have managed to disassociate from the events that made him even acknowledge the vicious atrocities, but, in a way, she was grateful because she now had a thorough understanding of the lengths that Sister Nora could go to.

She let out a shaky sigh and caught a glimpse of the little clock on the desk. She had been here for nearly thirty minutes. Mass would be ending soon, and she needed to put everything back in its place before Father Michael noticed anything had been moved. She blew out the candle, thrust the notebooks back inside the musty cabinet, and turned the key in the lock.

With the key still clenched in her hand, she sprinted back to the chapel, sending gravel flying around her in the process. She kicked the large stone which had been holding the office door open away from the building and jumped over the threshold. The door slammed shut behind her, and she cursed herself for making so much noise. If Father Michael asked, she would say she had opened the door to allow some fresh air in for him. She had just enough time to replace the key in his coat pocket and grab a nearby rag before he walked into the office.

She turned to greet him. 'Just finishing up, Father Michael. I'll be out of your way in a moment,' she said in a pleasant tone of voice.

Father Michael barely acknowledged her before heading past her into the room to change. *He really is a fool*, Katherine thought. *The place is still filthy, and he hasn't even noticed.*

Katherine threw away the dusty rag she had been holding and sauntered out the chapel door with a little pep in her step that terrified her. Given all that she knew now, it seemed wrong that she should be enthusiastic, but she was conflicted by the whole situation. She felt a sense of euphoria at having carried out her master plan with such success, but she was scared stiff about being stuck in an orphanage under the control of a possessed nun who seemed to have a keen interest in her. And there was no one she could trust or turn to for help within these walls. What was she to do now?

XII

It was now Sunday afternoon, and the last few days had passed by in a hazy blur for Katherine as she continued with her daily methodical routine. She was eager to keep a safe distance between herself and Father Michael, and so she threw herself fully into tackling the never-ending list of chores that Sister Nora gave her. If she kept her head down, she wouldn't draw any attention to herself.

Katherine was struggling to come to terms with what was happening around her. She could understand why she picked orphans as her victims of choice. In a country where over-crowding and a lack of state funding was common, and with no relatives to apply pressure, she imagined the state would turn a blind eye to the disappearance or death of some children in a remote orphanage.

Katherine was pruning a tree in the front garden. Stopping to stretch her aching back for a moment, she heard rapid foot-steps crunching on the gravel path nearby. She glanced up from her work and nearly jumped out of her skin. Sister Nora was standing right in front of her, her intimidating figure blocking out the sun. The nun's usually emotionless face was flushed and her breathing laboured. Her usually pristine heels were caked in thick mud and sludge. Katherine shivered.

'My office, Katherine. Now!' she barked at her through gritted teeth.

Katherine's stomach sank. She knew Sister Nora must have found out about her secret meeting with Father Michael. Why else would she be so furious?

She trudged across the gravel and through the cold hallway towards Sister Nora's office. She was tempted to run away but knew that would only make the situation worse. The last time she had been in Sister Nora's office, she left unable to walk, with scarred legs, and she hadn't even done anything to warrant the abuse. What punishment would she have to endure this time when Sister Nora had a viable reason to discipline her?

Sister Nora brushed past her into the office and beckoned with a deafening click of her fingers for Katherine to take a seat in the middle of the room, while she looked for something in the nearby press. A small, wheeled table covered with a dingy towel sat next to her chair. That hadn't been in the room last time she was there. She gripped the edge of the chair tightly, staring at the table. Whatever was underneath that towel was meant for her. The torture that had been documented in the notebooks flashed through her mind. She couldn't stop her knees from shaking.

Sister Nora closed the press with a heavy thud and returned to stand next to Katherine. She pulled on a pair of black rubber gloves, snapping them at the wrist. She had not even glanced in the direction of the shaking orphan or uttered a word, but her breathing had quickened, and her face was bright red with fury. She wheeled the table over so that it was right in front of her and whipped off the towel, revealing the sordid contents that lay beneath.

Katherine started to sob, her whole body shaking from panic.

On the table lay a variety of tools, some of which she had never seen before, but she did recognise a set of rusted forceps. She rose from her chair to try to reason with Sister Nora but all she received was a harsh slap across her cheek that silenced her and left a bright red handprint on her face.

'Was I not clear the last time I spoke with you? When I told you that you needed to learn your place? Did the pain in your legs not act as a reminder for your tiny brain of what would happen if you didn't comply?' Sister Nora asked, pushing Katherine back onto the chair.

Katherine began to stutter a weak explanation, but the words that came rushing from her mouth were almost incoherent.

'Nothing happens within these walls without my knowledge,' Sister Nora said, walking around Katherine, 'so I know all about your little secret meeting with Father Michael.'

Sister Nora had started to run her fingers across the old tools on the table while she was speaking, touching each one as if they were precious items. Katherine imagined she was savouring how the cold metal felt against her skin. Her hand eventually came to rest on one of the forceps. She snatched them up and passed them from one hand to the other like she was playing with them.

'Do you not like how I run things here? Does it scare you?' she scoffed. 'You're not the first one who has attempted to stand in my way here, to try to work out what I'm doing or why.'

Sister Nora suddenly stopped talking and sighed, as if the whole situation was exhausting for her. She halted in front of Katherine and closed her eyes. She smiled. When she opened her eyes again, they were black and empty. She raised her hands and grasped the crucifix, her knuckles growing white from the pressure, and she let out another deep sigh.

'I do these things because I *can*. I told you before, little Katherine, that I am the only God you need to know within these walls, and I am free to do whatever I want. No one can prove what I am doing here,' she said in a blunt manner. 'There is really no one outside this pitiful orphanage who cares enough to check on the wards of the state. You are all at my disposal. In fact, a few less mouths to feed here and there is probably a blessing for the country. I'm doing the country a justice. But I don't need to explain to you of all people what I get out of it,' Sister Nora said and chuckled.

Katherine looked up at her in fear and confusion.

'You won't admit it,' the nun went on, 'but I know you truly understand the feeling of getting away with certain acts. That sheer rush of being able to control the people around you, to have them obey your every command and dispose of them once they become useless.'

Sister Nora leaned down and put both her arms on the chair, trapping Katherine. She moved in close to Katherine's ear and whispered, 'You too have the Devil inside you.'

Katherine felt like her heart was about to leap from her chest. She had heard that statement only once before in her life. She didn't know if it was her fear that was making her hear things, but Sister Nora's voice had sounded exactly like her mother's.

Katherine glanced up at the face hovering above her, her heart beating in her chest. She was afraid of what she might see. She blinked twice to clear her vision, for it was her mother's face staring right back at her.

XIII

Katherine's mother had always been critical of her daughter. She couldn't accept that Katherine wasn't the traditional Catholic farm girl like the other girls in the village. She wasn't quiet and submissive like them, nor eager to please her parents. She was resourceful and cunning, wise beyond her years and able to get away with misdeeds. Money was always tight in their household, a fact her parents had pointed out to her ever since she was a young child, but that never stopped her from getting what she wanted.

It had started with pocketing some of Mrs Wilson's soda bread from the corner market stall whenever she passed after the service on Sundays. Her nimble actions meant she was long gone before Mrs Wilson had even noticed any of her stock was missing. The glee Katherine felt when she took a bite into that thick crust was indescribable. Why should she ever go without, when everything around her was for the taking? She could have anything she wanted. All she had to do was watch for opportunities as they presented themselves.

Of course, Katherine always tried to play the part of the virtuous daughter, but her mother never fell for her deception.

The collection of crumbs she often found in Katherine's coat pocket probably didn't help, but exposing Katherine's lies was only part of their difficult relationship. It was as if she could see through Katherine's mask of duplicity to what was really hidden in the depths of Katherine's soul.

As the extent of Katherine's lies grew over the years, so did her mother's fear of her. No punishment or restriction, no teaching of the difference between right and wrong, either morally or legally, made any difference. Looking back, Katherine could almost pinpoint the moment that her mother realised she would never be able to control her.

The event that caused Katherine's mother to understand her daughter's true nature was the mysterious disappearance of the village doctor's eight-year-old daughter, Michelle. As the only child of the esteemed doctor, she was spoiled by the villagers, so no one thought it odd that Katherine would befriend her even though she was a few years older.

Katherine thought she was the only one who saw Michelle for what she truly was – a spoilt, entitled crybaby, always carrying around a tattered little doll that her mother had knitted for her when she was a baby. She'd been born to a life of ease. Her blonde curly locks and bulbous face that was always red from crying made Katherine particularly vexed. *What reason could she have for crying all the time?* She didn't know the hardships of the real world … not yet.

Katherine was the last person to ever see Michelle alive. When the worried doctor knocked on the door of their home late that night, eager to locate his child, Katherine rattled off her well-rehearsed tale of how they'd been playing by the creek behind the church for most of the day. When it was time for Katherine to go home, Michelle had refused to leave, despite Katherine's desperate pleas that she would get into trouble if she wasn't home before dark.

But she didn't tell him what really happened to the half-witted Michelle. *They never did find her body, only the tattered little doll she carried around.*

The execution of her plan had almost been perfect. She hadn't anticipated her mother would arrive home early that evening. If she had only arrived ten minutes later, she would have never caught her hiding her bloodstained clothes by a pile of rocks near their well. Thankfully, her mother believed that 'blood was thicker than water', so she never told the police or the doctor what she saw.

After that, Katherine sensed her mother deliberately avoided her and began placing holy medals in every room of the house as a form of protection. But she still kept a watchful eye on her daughter. Then, in the spring, an incident occurred with a local village boy named Seamus Murphy.

Seamus was always fawning over Katherine, following her around and looking for her approval like a lost puppy. He tagged along with her and her friends as if he belonged with them. He seemed to think he was entitled to join them because the rest of the village decided he and Katherine were a perfect match and that there was an 'understanding' between the two families. Her family had been friends with his family for years, and his family had significant plots of land. Their union would protect the land for years to come, while also ensuring comfort for her own family for generations. Seamus' parents saw Katherine as a sort of carer for their dim-witted son, believing she would 'set him right' and give him enough children to take care of the farms.

Katherine thought Seamus was the definition of 'slow' and everything he did irritated her. He was rude and constantly spoke *at* her while refusing to listen to anything she had to say. He had lank, greasy hair and always smelt like the farm he worked on – a mixture of cow manure and mud. He went around wearing trousers that were always a bit too short for his legs, but he never seemed to notice despite the cool air freezing his exposed skin. And even though she'd never shown any interest in him, he would always call her his 'missus'. How could she ever consider him a match for her? But there would never be a marriage if Seamus was no longer alive!

The only good thing about his devotion was that he blindly did everything she wanted, which she used to her advantage.

She recalled one time when a neighbour's cat had a litter of kittens. They were lovely little things – all black and white and pottering around as they learnt to walk. Katherine, by her own admission, was a little jealous. She had always wanted a cat of her own, but her father had never allowed it. The old woman who owned the mother cat now had a whole litter for herself. It wasn't fair. Why should she have to go without?

The kittens' arrival provided her with the basis of an ingenious plan – a plan that would not only rid her of Seamus, but one that would also give the old woman what she deserved because she had the one thing Katherine wanted.

One evening, Katherine said to Seamus, 'If we are ever to be together, Seamus, I need to know that you'll do anything for me. That you'll provide for me. I really need those kittens. If you can't get them for me then I don't think I'll ever be able to marry you.'

'Will you really be my wife if I get you those kittens? Do you promise?' Seamus asked, the hopeful tone of his voice making Katherine nauseous. 'You can't break a promise, you know,' he said, pointing his finger at her, 'so if you promise me, you can't back out.'

You really are an idiot, she thought.

His eyes had lit up when she promised him. She even faked being excited about their future together. He hung on her every word; it was the only time she recalled him ever truly listening to her. It was all too easy to plant the devious seed in his head.

She told him to wait until everyone had gone to bed and that he couldn't tell a soul about their plan. People wouldn't understand. He promised he would return that night with the kittens so they could be together. Katherine had to stop herself from rolling her eyes in front of him. He was so pathetic.

Katherine slipped out that night to witness her plan in action. She knew Seamus would get caught quickly because he was too clumsy to remain undetected for long. What Katherine hadn't told Seamus was that the old woman's husband had failing eyesight and always slept with a shotgun by his bedside in case he was burgled. She'd learned this information when she'd eavesdropped on her parents who were good friends of their neighbours.

Perched on a nearby fence with her cloak wrapped tightly around her, Katherine swung her legs back and forth as she waited for the sound to go off. She could have only been there for about fifteen minutes when she heard frantic shouting followed by two echoing booms. She clasped her hands together, closed her eyes and threw her head back to the sky, relishing in her triumph. Her eyes shot open when the third gunshot went off. She hadn't been expecting a third shot. *Seamus must've really scared them when he broke into their house.* Katherine chuckled at the thought.

It wasn't long before the villagers came running out of their homes to see what the deafening noise had been. She heard the old woman screaming, so Katherine took that as her cue to head back home. She whistled as she skipped through an overgrown field. Her plan had worked! She'd gotten rid of Seamus and tainted the neighbours' cottage with the image of his dead body.

She ran into the kitchen laughing and congratulating herself to find her mother sitting at the table, under the dim glow of a small candle. Her shoulders were slumped, and her eyes were wide and glassy.

She didn't have to ask her what happened, the distant screaming and the jovial look on Katherine's face gave everything away. Her mother only spoke one sentence to her before she leapt to her feet and backed out of the room. She didn't ask for any explanation but said in a low voice, 'You, my girl, have the Devil within you.' It was a statement that had stayed with Katherine over the years. Shortly after, the threats of being sent to the Convent of Mercy began.

Katherine didn't care. She had managed to get what she wanted – to be rid of Seamus. She'd never made it a secret that she didn't want to marry Seamus, but nobody listened to her or told him to back off. What she wanted didn't matter to them. Seamus was an idiot, and she didn't see anything wrong with ridding herself of an imbecile who wouldn't leave her alone.

She didn't shed a tear at Seamus' funeral, nor did she defend him when people called him a vandal for breaking into the house. She was proud of herself for having sorted out her problem on her own, but unfortunately, she never did get that kitten. And that was the real tragedy in her eyes.

Back in the present, Katherine shut her eyes and shook her head, desperate to get away from the memories of her haunting old life. Her mother was long dead, so she knew that her mind must have been playing tricks on her. She couldn't be here looking at her. When she reopened them, Sister Nora's black eyes stared right back, piercing through her.

'You talk too much, Katherine; you are too loose with your words, and your inability to fall in line is growing problematic for me. I would have thought our last discussion would have penetrated that thick skull of yours with the importance of staying out of my business,' she said, jabbing her finger at Katherine's temple. 'But perhaps we need to try a harsher approach to make the message sink in. Open your mouth.'

Katherine vehemently shook her head, every instinct in her body was telling her to keep her mouth clamped shut.

'Open your mouth, or I will open it for you!' Sister Nora barked. She dropped her arms from the chair and Katherine saw her opportunity.

She leapt up and tried to run to the door, but Sister Nora managed to intercept her and drag her back to the chair with an inhuman strength. Then, she lunged at Katherine, pulling her hair back and ripping out some chunks in the process. She forced her head back so that it was facing upwards and used the forceps to make her mouth remain open. If Katherine tried to close her mouth, she would only taste rusted metal and probably destroy her teeth.

Sister Nora remined still for a few moments, then began tapping the forceps across each tooth while staring menacingly at her. 'Which tooth should I go for first?' she said, her eyes gleaming as she taunted the young girl.

Katherine's eyes were wide with fear, and she could barely see Sister Nora through her tears. Her pupils kept darting back and forth between Sister Nora's face and the forceps, trying to gauge when she would pounce, hoping to brace for the impact. She could see how the nun was enjoying the extent of the power she had over her, knowing there was nothing Katherine could do to stop what was coming.

'You are stuck here, Katherine,' she said, breathing harshly into her face, 'and I will not tolerate anyone meddling in my affairs. You think you are all holier-than-thou, going behind my back to Father Michael … and to find out what, exactly? Answers to questions which you already knew? You knew what happened to those girls. Come on now, Katherine, aren't you meant to be smart? Did you really believe that the body you saw on your first day was due to natural causes?'

Sister Nora scoffed and rolled her eyes. 'What exactly were you planning to do once you'd got those answers? Did you think you could find solace in Father Michael? That he was going to save you? That little idiot will be no help to you. He does as I say, just like everyone else within these walls. Blood will continue to be shed within this place for as long as I wish. It is my kingdom to do with as I please, and all of you are disposable beings, like trash.'

Unexpectedly, Sister Nora loosened her tight grip on Katherine's hair. She retreated slowly, like a snake slithering back into its hole, and stood in front of the gasping orphan, twisting the forceps around in her hand.

Katherine couldn't believe it. Had Sister Nora decided to let her go after all? Was this all just to teach her a lesson? She tried to pull herself together as best she could. She straightened herself up and swiped her tears away. Then she remembered her previous vow – to never show fear in Sister Nora's presence. She glared at her through narrowed eyes and sniffed, then used the back of her hand to wipe her nose. She was angry with herself for having succumbed to her fear. In an instant, she had undone her promise to herself. She would've kicked herself if she could.

As if sensing Katherine's anger and frustration, Sister Nora smirked. Her free hand reached up to brush against the crucifix, and she shook her head, her face contorted in a twisted grin as a maniacal chuckle emerged. She lunged towards Katherine, who was flung backwards off her chair. Her back slammed into the wooden floor, and the chair clattered to the side. Winded, Katherine didn't have time to register what was happening as Sister Nora straddled her and perched on her chest.

Katherine didn't have enough strength left to push the nun off her body. Her weak arms could only hit at the nun's legs, a futile attempt as Sister Nora didn't even register the impact. And the nun's weight made it difficult for her to breathe, so she couldn't even let out a desperate cry for help.

Suddenly, she could breathe momentarily as Sister Nora leaned forward, thrust the forceps into Katherine's mouth and pulled out one of her back molars, slicing through her tongue in the process.

Blood gushed forth and the pain made her head spin. Sister Nora sat back on her chest, restricting her breath once more. She held up the stolen molar to the light and smiled. Katherine could make out part of her gum still attached to the end of the tooth. She began to cough, the thick red blood spluttering from her mouth, but Sister Nora just leaned over her and smiled.

The last thing Katherine saw before she passed out was the glint of the crucifix as it fell from Sister Nora's neck and dangled over her face.

XIV

The next morning, Katherine awoke sweating in her bed. She didn't know how she had managed to get back to her room, but she guessed that Sister Nora must have called upon Father Michael to take her back to her room once she had finished with her. It took Katherine a few moments to take in her surroundings and then the true horror of the events of the evening prior came flooding back to her. Overcome by the shock of it, her tears started to spill. She gingerly made her way from her bed to the murky mirror hanging on the adjacent wall. She had to stretch up on her tiptoes to see her reflection in the glass, but once her face came into view, she barely recognised the reflection staring back at her.

Her hair was knotted and raggedy, and her scalp was red raw from the clumps of hair that Sister Nora had ripped from her. Her complexion was that of a ghost – pale and gaunt – and she looked almost ill. She inched her hand up to touch the side of her face but recoiled only a few seconds later due to the intense pain she felt in her mouth when her hand touched her cheek. She leaned in closer to the mirror and forced herself to open her mouth to get a better look at the damage that had been done. The side of her tongue was swollen, and the cut was deep from the forceps. There was a gaping dark hole at the back of her gum which was still bleeding from where her tooth once was.

She was in disbelief, as if trapped in a nightmare that wouldn't end. Despite the pain, she moved her tongue tentatively across the rest of her mouth to make sure Sister Nora hadn't destroyed anything else when she'd passed out.

She sank down to the floor in despair and rested her head upon her knees. The floors were cold against her skin, but she would rather focus on that than the searing pain she could feel in her face. She knew from everything she had learnt that some orphans who had come up against the malicious nun weren't as lucky as she was – to make it out of her office alive. Why had Sister Nora chosen to toy with her, rather than ending her life? If she was such a threat to her grand plan, why keep her around? It was difficult to feel relieved about being alive when she was stuck in the orphanage with this madwoman until she became eighteen. *That is, if I survive to become eighteen*, she thought. She felt like an animal trapped inside a cage with its predator. It may have been easier for her if Sister Nora had just ended everything there, but it was evident why she had chosen to torture her instead. Sister Nora didn't want to make things easier for Katherine. She wanted to make her every minute filled with terror and pain. It was all a game of power to her.

Katherine closed her eyes and tried to take a deep breath but, as soon as her eyelids shut, all she could see was the crucifix hanging over her face. She forced herself to open her eyes and shook her head in a frenzy from side to side, trying to get rid of the haunting imagery from her mind. If this whole situation taught her anything, it was that Sister Nora wasn't fully human. Up until she came to the orphanage, she didn't even know of this woman, and she was certain that her family hadn't either. However, Sister Nora knew about a conversation that she had had privately with her mother, word for word, as if she had been there right next to them when it happened. She had even managed to mimic her mother's voice, a sound she herself hadn't heard in months. No human could know these things or be able to mimic someone's voice so profoundly.

It was clear that Sister Nora was being controlled by an inhuman entity that was giving her unexplainable power. Father Michael had said it was the Devil, but he also said that evil lies within everyone, so maybe this was who Sister Nora really was. Perhaps *she* was the evil entity, and the crucifix was simply letting her true nature be shown. Katherine was both intrigued and terrified by the sheer, incomprehensible force being projected from this mysterious crucifix into the vessel that was Sister Nora.

What was she to do now? Sister Nora was right from the very start; she was stuck here. She had no one to check up on her wellbeing. Her friends had long since forgotten about her since her parents' funeral. They hadn't even called to see her before she was sent to the orphanage.

She scoffed. 'Some friends they were,' she said aloud.

The way she saw it, she only had a few options at her disposal, but none of them were optimal. Katherine dragged herself up from the floor and paced the room as she weighed up her options.

'I could wait until everyone in the orphanage goes to bed for the night, pack my bag, and run away. I could leave all of this horror behind me and start fresh somewhere,' she muttered under her breath.

But then what? Where would I go? Nobody will believe the extravagant tales of an orphan, especially when the story seems too far-fetched to be true. And who could blame them, if I wasn't living this nightmare myself, I wouldn't believe it either if someone came crying to me with stories of the Devil and a cursed crucifix.'

She raised her hands in frustration. She had no money and minimal prospects. She would be forced to wander the cold, disease-filled streets, picking pockets to survive, unless she was fortunate enough to catch a fever and pass away.

Her other option was to go to a church and try to seek sanctuary there, but given Father Michael's deception she was wary of trusting another supposed 'Man of God'. What if there was the same evil there too? What if it followed her? What would happen if Sister Nora ended up finding her? The only other option was to remain in the orphanage with Sister Nora for three more years, until she could leave.

If she kept quiet and minded her own business, then surely it would lessen the routine torture that Sister Nora directed at her. There were always new orphans arriving and, maybe in a few days' time, a new arrival might become fixed in Sister Nora's sights. If she was no longer on her radar, if another orphan had done worse things than she had, then the tirade would have to stop. However, this idea didn't sit well with Katherine. Her chest tightened and her stomach twisted at the thought.

To have another orphan in her exact position meant that she would have to act oblivious, knowing that Sister Nora would be inflicting this insane torture on someone who could end up being a lot younger and more fragile than Katherine. If she were to do this, then she would be no better than Father Michael.

She shook her head in defeat. 'I can't do that. These children have done nothing wrong. They don't deserve to be subjected to that,' Katherine muttered as she walked over to the window and gazed out.

She didn't want to become as spineless as he was, especially when some of the orphans were quite young and might not be strong enough to survive the unending abuse. But to not turn a blind eye meant that she would forever be subjecting herself to bouts of sadistic torture simply because Sister Nora can, and she felt like she deserved it.

Katherine's mind was frazzled with the culmination of her opposing thoughts and emotions. She kept changing from feeling sorry for herself to being angry. She was livid with her parents. Had they not died, or had they put a solid plan in place in case they died prematurely, she wouldn't even be here.

She hated that her parents had been so stuck in their own little passive world of tending to the farm and going ritually to mass that they failed to prepare for any sort of future, a future which they were now destined to no longer have. One that they denied Katherine of. Through the tears cascading down her face, Katherine managed to laugh, not out of humour or relief but out of the sheer desperation of the situation.

She had no choice; that was crystal clear. She had to stay here and try to survive as best she could. She didn't wish her pain and suffering to be projected on another orphan, but she had to put herself first and watch her own back. She would have to remain invisible and wouldn't try to make friends with anyone. If Sister Nora saw that she was getting too comfortable, she couldn't guarantee the safety of those around her. Instead, she would take on extra chores to help each day pass quicker, giving her something productive to focus on, rather than the hell and immense pain of every day. She would no longer go looking for answers. She knew everything she needed to know now and if she were to ever get that itching feeling to go deeper with that knowledge or to expose the evil within the walls of the orphanage, well then, her sliced tongue and severed gum would act as a permanent reminder of what would happen to her if she were to ever disobey the word of Sister Nora again. She needed to keep in her place. That was all that mattered now.

XV

The weeks crawled by as winter gave way to spring, and Katherine kept to her word. She kept herself busy by taking on new chores in the scullery and being diligent in carrying them out, avoiding giving Sister Nora any reason to target her. This worked quite well for a while, but after a short period of time it seemed Sister Nora was growing tired of not having any legitimate reason to hurt Katherine. Despite her perfect behaviour, on more than one occasion, she found herself back in the confines of Sister Nora's office, holding back tears as she received lash after lash from her extensive range of riding crops. No matter what she did, she couldn't escape her wrath.

Every few days or so, more orphans unfortunately met their demise. It was frightening how Katherine had grown accustomed to the endless passing faces in the building. Given the sadistic pattern of the nun, seeing a face one day at dinner and having an empty spot in their assigned seat at breakfast the next morning was something that Katherine had quickly learnt to accept as normal. Father Michael had even constructed a new makeshift graveyard on the other side of the building to keep up with the disposal of the ever-increasing number of bodies. As he scuttled around the gardens, Katherine couldn't help but imagine how fast those notebooks of his must have been filling up.

She had made the fatal error one morning of offering a welcoming smile to a newcomer called Rachel. She couldn't help it, Rachel's doe-like face made it impossible for her to maintain her cold, stone-like nature. Rachel returned a sheepish smile to her and, for the first time in what felt like years, Katherine felt a small stirring of warmth in her body.

However, Rachel didn't appear for lunch that afternoon; her seat remained empty. A look of puzzlement crossed Katherine's face as she looked around the room, trying to catch a glimpse of her, on the off-chance that Rachel had simply chosen to sit somewhere else. She caught sight of Sister Nora at the head table with a wicked smirk on her face, twisting the crucifix in her hand as she observed Katherine's discomfort. Katherine guessed that Rachel had joined the unfortunate list of Sister Nora's victims. She knew if she were to head out into the graveyard, she would see a freshly dug hole in the ground.

Father Michael was right; no matter what she did, Sister Nora would be watching her, targeting her, ensuring she and those around her would suffer excruciating pain and anguish. Anyone who came close or appeared to be friendly towards her wasn't safe.

Katherine began to struggle with the idea of remaining isolated and alone until she turned eighteen. Her desperation became too much to handle, and her sadness began to consume her. This, of course, only seemed to lighten Sister Nora's mood. Katherine couldn't sleep without seeing images of Sister Nora's smirking face and the gleaming beacon of the crucifix invading her dreams. She stopped eating and her eyes became deep, hollow, sunken pits in her face. She had stopped looking up altogether, afraid to meet anyone's gaze for fear that

Sister Nora would interpret this as a form of comradery and would decide to end their time in this world.

As a way of trying to cope with the insanity, to keep herself grounded and not feel so lonely, she had chosen to put all her time and energy into counting her steps. To the outsider, it may have seemed a little unorthodox, but counting her steps gave her something else to focus on other than her desperate situation. She now knew it took her precisely four hundred and seventy-one steps to make it from her bedroom to the chapel and three hundred and twelve steps to the dining room. It had become a sort of game; each day she wanted to lessen the number of steps it took her to reach her destination, and she felt annoyed with herself if she failed to do so. It was the only thing helping her to hold on to her sanity and to remain lucid.

One Sunday afternoon, following the twelve o'clock service in the chapel, she was walking back to her dorm, her gaze fixated on her feet, counting each step as usual. As she was nearing the gravel path near the main building, a pair of worn, faded black shoes came into view and stopped her in her tracks. She tentatively looked up. She knew that it couldn't be Sister Nora; she wouldn't stoop to wearing unpolished shoes. But who else would be coming to speak with her? She was surprised to see the weathered face of Sister Sorcha – the nun who had made eye contact with her on her very first day in the orphanage. She had never heard the nun speak, and she had heard some of the girls mocking her because she was mute.

She sidestepped the elderly nun, afraid of anyone being seen near her, but Sister Sorcha sidestepped with her, blocking her path. Katherine looked down at the gravel. She didn't know why Sister Sorcha wasn't letting her pass but if her history with Sister Nora was anything to go by, she didn't think it wise to trust her intentions. Sister Sorcha reached down, attempting to grasp Katherine's hands which were still puffy and cut from her last encounter with Sister Nora. Katherine glanced up at the woman and tried to move her hands behind her back, out of fear and embarrassment, but with a gentleness she wasn't expecting, the nun grabbed Katherine's wrists, stopping her from moving.

Sister Sorcha didn't flinch when she saw how deep the cuts on Katherine's hands were. She pulled out a thin, brown gauze which she had concealed under the sleeve of her habit and bound Katherine's wounds, being careful not to cause her any more pain in the process. Katherine couldn't remember the last time she had experienced such a display of kindness from someone and couldn't help the tears which were beginning to pool in her eyes. Sister Sorcha lowered her head so that she was looking straight into Katherine's eyes. Her eyes were tender and unyielding, a stark difference from the empty, dead eyes of Sister Nora. Sorcha glanced around, her head darting everywhere, checking to make sure no one was witnessing their caring exchange, and gently cupped Katherine's cheek, wiping away her tears in the process. Her hands were warm against Katherine's frozen face, and she couldn't help but lean into her touch. It was comforting to her and reminded her of the way her mother used to treat her when she was a young child.

A nearby flock of crows suddenly flew over the chapel spire, startled by something. They were making a lot of noise, cawing as they went, which disrupted the tender moment. Sister Sorcha dropped her hand and stepped back. She offered Katherine a fleeting half-smile that struggled to fully reach her eyes and slowly shuffled towards the chapel as if nothing had ever happened.

It was a few minutes later before Katherine was able to breathe again. She hadn't realised she'd been holding her breath for the duration of their interaction. She turned around to face the direction in which Sister Sorcha had gone, in disbelief that a moment like that could happen to her here, but the nun was long gone. She raised her hand to try to savour the feeling of warmth on her cheek. Katherine kicked at a nearby stone and smiled. She didn't know how to deal with the positive feelings running through her. It was the first time she'd smiled in weeks.

She shuffled her way back towards the main building. She was confused as she had never had any encounter with Sister Sorcha before, other than a quick glance. Her kindness made her feel like, at last, there was someone in the orphanage she could turn to, someone who may become a friend. They were both outcasts – Katherine because of her association with Sister Nora and her isolation, and Sorcha because she was different from the rest of the nuns. Being mute clearly put a barrier between her and the others. In a way, they were destined to be friends because their misery connected them. Katherine was conflicted though. The last time she thought she could trust someone, she had been viciously attacked, causing her to lose a tooth and ending up with a grotesque, sliced tongue that she would be stuck with forever. Perhaps their interaction had been a one-off moment. She almost hoped so. If Sister Nora suspected that someone was being kind to her, then both herself and that person would face her wrath.

Katherine allowed herself, for a moment, to relish in the brief level of kindness she was shown. With a heavy heart, she resigned herself to the simple fact that it was just for that one time. She trudged up the steep steps and over the threshold of the door. Her newly bound hands hurt just a little less due to the bandages. She ran her hands along the wooden banister of the stairs, replaying Sister Sorcha's act of kindness in her head as she went. However, she couldn't stop the nagging feeling that someone was behind her, watching her as she moved. She was used to Sister Nora appearing from nowhere like a menacing phantom, but she still didn't want to be caught by surprise. She turned around, her heart pounding in her chest, but there was no one there. She ran back to the musty corner of the hall, right back to the banister from which she had just come. She glanced around in case someone had followed her without her knowing and had yet to make themselves known. She raced down a few steps just to make sure, but there was no one around. She went back up the few stairs which she had just come down from, clumsily tripping over the last one in the process. She had to put her hands out in front of her to stop herself from falling to the ground and hitting her face. She winced as soon as she felt the impact on her hands; the gauze wasn't thick enough to shield her hands from the pain of that.

She cursed herself at her own stupidity, shaking her hands to get rid of the pain, and skulked into her bedroom. She tried to shrug off her nerves and paranoia but couldn't shake the feeling she was being watched. She grabbed the rosary beads that were lying in a tangled heap on her desk and prayed hard for Sister Sorcha, hoping that nothing harmful would come to such a kind soul. She clasped her hands tightly together, ignoring the searing pain that was shooting up through her body. Her knuckles strained with tension, a stark contrast against her skin as she clutched them tightly, but she paid no attention; instead, she prayed that Sister Nora hadn't seen her encounter with Sister Sorcha. If she hadn't, the nun would remain safe.

She looked up to the heavens in desperation and began to repeat, 'Saint Michael the Archangel, defend us in battle. Be our protection against the wickedness and snares of the Devil. May God rebuke him, we humbly pray; and do thou, O Prince of the heavenly host, by the power of God, thrust into hell Satan and all of the other evil spirits who prowl about the world seeking the ruin of souls. Amen.'

XVI

When Tuesday arrived, the orphanage was in absolute turmoil. The orphans were instructed to go about their chores and routine prayers as normal, but there was a heavy air of tension, and everyone was on edge, waiting for Sister Nora to snap. Apparently, the convent had had a surprise visitor the previous night. From her window, Katherine had noticed the arrival of a muddied trap and horse before she went to bed around eleven o'clock. She knew it must have been an unexpected visitor as no one ventured to the convent that late in the night.

One of the young girls, who was now lying cold in a hole in the ground, under an unmarked grave, had a distant uncle who the state hadn't been aware of when she was first charged into the care of the orphanage. He had been overseas in America when his brother had passed, so hadn't heard the news until he returned home, months after the funeral. He had been trying to find his niece for weeks and now, at long last, had landed on the steps of the convent to retrieve her and bring her back home with him. Hut having arrived so late in the night, he had been instructed by Father Michael to return the following morning, at a more reasonable hour.

Sister Nora was rattled as she awaited his arrival. Nobody had seen her this shaken before, fidgeting and muttering under her breath as she paced the floors. Everyone was walking on eggshells around her, afraid in case they would be the one to set off her towering rage. An outsider had never come to look for a child who had been placed in her care before.

Katherine saw her that morning, moving in a frenzy throughout the convent in anticipation of the mysterious uncle's arrival. The crucifix, which was usually displayed with pride on top of her habit, was hidden underneath. Katherine knew she was still wearing it because the top of the gold chain was visible above her collar. Animated hushed whispers were heard in the dark corners of the room between Sister Nora and Father Michael, and he too was moving in a panic throughout the place, preparing for the visitor.

The rest of the nuns seemed to be on edge too. Their total silence was unsettling, and they were all determined to keep out of Sister Nora's path. It was obvious that they weren't quite sure what to do with themselves. Some were clutching their rosary beads to their chests as if their lives depended on it, muttering pleas to God under their breath as they walked. Others were simply erratic as they moved about the room, unable to sit still for too long, while making sure that if Sister Nora passed them, they directed their eyes anywhere else and jumped out of her path.

Katherine had been applying beeswax to the doorframes in the main living room at this time. She was feeling oddly optimistic about this visitor. Surely now, every sordid detail – the abuse, murder and deception – would come to light. There was no way she could explain the mysterious disappearance of the girl who had been in her care. Maybe this was the twist of luck that Katherine had long been waiting for. She wouldn't have to put up with the tiresome exploits of Sister Nora for much longer. Surely the state would have to become involved. They wouldn't be able to turn a blind eye to the horrors of the orphanage anymore. With Sister Nora's every move being scrutinised, she wouldn't be able to carry out her horrific atrocities anymore.

Katherine breathed a sigh of relief as she carried on polishing. Everything would be alright once this day was over. However, she dared not look up from her work in case she managed to draw Sister Nora's attention. She knew that the moments before and after the visit would be the most dangerous for the girls in the orphanage. Sister Nora would be seething once the uncle left and would be looking to inflict pain on whoever happened to be in her line of vision. They would be living in the eye of the storm until either the officials intervened or Sister Nora snapped.

Having finished her task, Katherine stood up and rolled her shoulders. They cracked and ached from the act of leaning down for so long. She took a step back to assess her work and accidentally stood upon someone in the process. Her eyes went wide in fear and her heart stopped. Thinking it may have been Sister Nora, Katherine dropped her cloth and shrunk back, nearly tripping over her own feet in the process. A firm hand reached out to steady her before she fell over, and Katherine recognised the warmth of the frail hands of Sister Sorcha right away. Despite her anxiety, she let out a nervous chuckle, letting it fall short in case anyone else around heard her. Sister Sorcha picked up the rag that Katherine had been holding and handed it back to the shaking girl in front of her. She offered her an amused smile and pursed her lips as if to say 'Really?', and carried on walking into the room. Katherine looked after her fondly, so consumed within her own thoughts that she hadn't even noticed she was being watched.

From the dark recesses of the room Sister Nora's dark eyes had narrowed into menacing slits. Her movements were robotic as she reached her hand up towards the hidden chain around her neck, her jaw clenching as she did so.

'What a fool,' she whispered under her breath.

'Katherine really won't listen. Vile vermin like her should remain isolated and alone. She doesn't deserve any friendship.'

She scoffed. 'Does she honestly think that weak Sister Sorcha is going to be the light for her in this place? There can be no friends here, no solidarity. I've made that perfectly clear. I thought Sister Sorcha knew the consequences of going against my wishes, but it's clear the message hasn't sunk in as deep as I thought. Perhaps,' she muttered as she paced the room, 'their budding friendship could be the most effective way of ensuring that Katherine understands her place and stays within it. It would destroy her soul if she knew that her friend was taken from her because of her actions.'

The shrill ring of the bell pulled her from her malicious trance.

'I'll deal with them later. Right now, there's a bigger issue to contend with.'

The uncle arrived, and everyone held their breath in fearful anticipation, afraid to be the one to set Sister Nora off. She straightened her back and moved with grace towards the main door. Oddly enough, all the tension had disappeared from her face, and she seemed quite relaxed. It was as if she had put on a mask, hiding her true feelings and self from the visitor. Katherine peered around the side of the door, trying to make out what was happening. She didn't want to miss a minute of this cumbersome interaction. The uncle was standing in the hallway with obvious discomfort, looking around, trying to survey his surroundings. He was a relatively young man, no more than thirty-two years old, Katherine guessed. He was clean-shaven, with muddy-brown hair, and was wearing an oversized tweed jacket that she thought might have belonged to someone else, based on how ill-fitting it was.

He twisted his flat cap between his hands and his face was flushed and sweaty. Katherine guessed he was a working man – judging by his bulky and calloused hands.

Sister Nora exchanged words with the uncle who suddenly got quite agitated, flaying his arms around him in anger. Sister Nora directed him to walk ahead of her, down the hallway, towards her office. He shook his head and stomped off in the direction in which he'd just been directed. Sister Nora paused and looked at Katherine, giving her a twisted smirk and shaking her index finger at her, before she strutted off after the uncle.

After what felt like an eternity later, they both emerged from the office. Sister Nora, to Katherine's surprise, smiled sympathetically and shook the uncle's hand. This wasn't the outcome Katherine had been expecting. She knitted her eyebrows together in puzzlement and continued to watch their interaction. She strained her ears to hear what was being said, but she only managed to make out the final words between them.

'I'm so sorry I couldn't be of more help, Mr Coleman. If there is ever anything I or this convent can do for you, please do not hesitate to reach out. God will be watching over you,' Sister Nora said, as she extended her hand to him.

The uncle gave her a short nod, pulled on his flat cap, and stepped through the main door. He stopped, before closing the door behind him, to glance at the sheepish orphans who were observing from a safe distance. Katherine saw tears in his eyes, but he didn't look angry. Instead, his interaction with Sister Nora showed there was no ill blood between the two of them. *What the hell did she say to him in her office?* she thought.

Her head began to spin. This was not what she thought would happen. She had been expecting screaming and shouting, and policemen being called to the scene, but there was none of that. Everything was eerily calm and contained, and Sister Nora appeared unaffected by the meeting. What was going on?

The atmosphere was tense as everyone waited for the expected explosion from Sister Nora, but it never came. As the orphans continued to watch on with apprehension, Sister Nora strode towards the window in the drawing room, pulling back the curtain with one finger so she could peer out. Katherine assumed she was watching Mr Coleman to make sure he had left the grounds. Once satisfied, Sister Nora spun on her heel to face the anxious orphans in the room. She looked at them and sighed.

'Children, Mr Coleman has been ill advised. It's quite tragic really,' she scoffed. 'A local townswoman had told him tales – that his niece, Jane, was being cared for here at the Convent of Mercy. Let us hope the poor woman was simply confused and not fabricating malicious lies.'

She stopped for a few seconds, making eye contact with many of them as she emphasised her next point.

'We know that lying is one of the deadly sins and she will be punished for that. Having gone through all the admissions paperwork both past and present with him and finding no evidence of us having taken in any girl called Jane, Mr Coleman has apologised for taking up our valuable time and won't be bothering us again. Isn't that just simply wonderful?' said Sister

Nora with a tone of fake optimism as she moved to stand next to the fireplace.

A heavy silence descended upon the place. Katherine knew that Mr Coleman hadn't been wrong. She had met Jane herself; everyone had. It explained the whispers between Father Michael and Sister Nora that morning; there would be no paperwork to prove the girl's existence within this sad excuse of a sanctuary. Between the power of the crucifix and the Devil, and the questionable skills of Father Michael presumably with gasoline and a matchbox, Sister Nora had managed to evade any repercussions for her actions. She had committed a saddened man to continue looking for his niece, knowing full well that she was no longer walking the earth. Katherine shook her head in disgust. Today was to be the day it was meant to all end – when justice was would prevail, and good would triumph over evil. But once again, the darkness reigned in this godless place.

Katherine saw Sister Sorcha bless herself before walking towards the door. She placed her hand on Katherine's shoulder, a quick yet comforting interaction between the two of them, as she passed. The light that had been shining through the narrow window suddenly dimmed. Katherine turned around to find the source and saw Sister Nora standing there. She tilted her head and folded her arms as she smirked at Katherine. The crucifix was now proudly displayed like a malevolent beacon in its usual spot on her chest.

Katherine's heart started pounding in her chest. Sister Nora had seen Sorcha's gesture of comfort. The nun stalked towards her and placed her hand right where Sister Sorcha had placed hers, eliminating any level of warmth that had been there. A shiver raked its way through Katherine's body. She was ice-cold and frozen in her spot. Sister Nora brought her index finger up and shook it back and forth, scolding Katherine like a petulant toddler. Then she looked in the direction in which the mute nun had gone and back at Katherine, making sure she understood: Sister Sorcha was now her next target.

'My office, Katherine. Tonight,' Sister Nora said in a cutting tone as she stalked away in Sister Sorcha's wake.

Katherine shuddered again. There was no escaping being punished that night. Sister Nora had made it crystal clear that she wanted Katherine's loneliness to consume her until it was the only thing she could think of. She wanted to kill any level of hope and optimism she was clinging to until she was just a shell of a human, scarred by abuse. However, Katherine was more focused on what would happen to Sorcha. She would heal from whatever torture Sister Nora inflicted upon her, but Sister Sorcha was gentle and frail, and she wouldn't even be able to cry out or call for help if she needed to. She would be totally in the hands of a cursed madwoman.

She wanted to run off in search of Sorcha, to protect her and keep her safe if she could, but she knew that this was just not possible. If Sister Nora had a target in mind, then there was nothing stopping her from inflicting pain on them. Nothing would ever stand in her way. If Sister Nora found her trying to warn her, she knew the outcome would only end up being worse for the both of them. Katherine turned around and with a heavy reluctance, returned to her chores, swallowing back a large lump in her throat. She really hoped there wouldn't be an empty seat where Sister Sorcha usually sat at dinner that evening.

XVII

Later that evening, Katherine was waiting for the dinner bell, her stomach in knots as her anxiety grew. She hadn't seen Sister Nora or Sister Sorcha since the dreaded visit that afternoon. She didn't know how severe Sister Sorcha's injuries were, or worse, if she was dead. She drummed her fingers across her desk, her leg hopping up and down with anticipation. At last, the ding of the bell rang, and all the orphans gathered to descend on the dining room. Katherine forced her way past the group of girls, pushed her way to the front of the queue and took her seat at the table. Once everyone was seated and silent, the procession of the nuns began.

Katherine strained her neck to try to make out if Sister Sorcha was one of them and sure enough, in the middle of the line-up, there she was. Katherine let out a deep sigh of relief and allowed herself to relax a bit. Sister Sorcha was alive. That was the main thing.

She squinted, trying to make out if there were any obvious injuries on the woman. The right-hand side of Sorcha's face appeared to have a tinge of blue and her top lip was split, but she couldn't be certain; it looked like she had used powder on her face to mask the true extent of the damage.

Sister Sorcha didn't make eye contact, keeping her head down just like the other nuns. Katherine started to bite her nails, as her heart raced. She wanted to make sure Sorcha was alright, to offer the woman some level of comfort, to return the gesture she had received herself. The fact that the nun didn't even look over at her made her worry. Had she lost the only comrade she ever had in the orphanage? She cast a fleeting glance at Sister Nora, who was grinning at her.

She's enjoying this, thought Katherine. *She likes that she's blocked our friendship. Sorcha won't ever go against her now, not when she'll be subjected to pain if she does.*

Defeated, Katherine shrank back in her seat. She wanted to disappear. With shaking hands, she gingerly picked up a spoon and forced herself to eat the bowl of mush that they called dinner.

The next morning, Katherine gasped as she plunged her hands deep into the basin of warm soapy water. The lashings she'd received from Sister Nora the night before had left her with deep lacerations along her spine, making her grit her teeth with every movement she made, but she had no choice but to carry on. Her hands were red and stinging from the heat of the water as she pulled out another frock. She had been scheduled for laundry duty and she still had about twenty more frocks to wash before she could hang them out to dry. She always hated laundry; it had been the one chore that she had always refused to help her mother with. She hated how tiring it was, to run the clothing over the board multiple times, then wring out each item which was saturated with murky water.

Her father's clothes were even worse as they were heavier than both her mother's and hers combined. They also reeked of cheap whiskey and tobacco, so she had to scrub at the material a lot harder to get rid of the foul stench. Her fingers became all wrinkly and red and sometimes sore and cracked from the pressure of pushing the clothes against the hard wooden board.

With a frustrated sigh, she pushed her hair back from her face with the back of her hand before wringing out the excess water from the frock into a nearby basin. She was so occupied by her thoughts about her task that she hadn't noticed someone else had entered the room. She went back to her little stool when she felt the all too familiar warmth of a comforting hand on her shoulder.

Tears sprang from the corners of Katherine's eyes, threatening to cascade down her face. She hadn't lost her only friend after all. Wiping her wet hands on her apron, she turned to face the woman behind her. Katherine gasped and brought her hands up to cover her mouth.

Sister Sorcha wasn't wearing any powder today. Katherine could see exactly what Sister Nora had done to her. Her top lip was split and the blueish tinge that she noticed at dinner yesterday was almost purple in patches. From the size of the discolouration on Sorcha's face, Katherine guessed Sister Nora had used a blunt object as her mode of punishment.

Instinctively, Katherine reached out to touch her face, but Sister Sorcha shrank back and closed her eyes as if in fear of the anticipated pain. Katherine retracted her hand and looked down in embarrassment, scolding herself for her stupidity.

Katherine swallowed a lump in her throat. 'I am so sorry, Sister Sorcha. This is all my fault,' she said.

The nun raised her hand to stop her from saying anything further, then moved with stealth towards the large brass taps at the opposite side of the room. She turned all of them on, before turning to face Katherine and putting her finger over her lips.

Katherine frowned, puzzled. The nun pointed upstairs, and Katherine understood. Someone was walking around upstairs and, judging by the unfaltering footsteps, she knew Sister Nora was standing right above them and that, for their sake, they needed to remain quiet.

'I'm so sorry, Sister,' whispered Katherine.

The nun shook her head and pulled Katherine into a comforting hug. Katherine froze before melting into the kind woman's arms. She smelt distinctly of frankincense, so Katherine guessed she must have come directly from the chapel, but there was also a hint of sage that Katherine had begun to associate with the woman.

'You're afraid of her too, aren't you?' Katherine asked while toying with her hands.

The frail nun was on edge; she kept looking around the room, checking it was safe to talk. She reluctantly nodded her head and gestured for the young girl to take a seat.

The nun pulled an empty basin next to Katherine to provide a makeshift seat for herself. The sheer fear that was written on Sister Sorcha's face made Katherine reluctant to probe the woman further, but she almost couldn't help herself.

'What else has she done to you?' Katherine asked, as she placed a gentle hand upon the woman's knee.

A silent tear made its way down Sister Sorcha's face as she seemed to be struggling with opening her mouth. This puzzled Katherine as she couldn't understand why the nun would even be trying to open her mouth in the first place when she was a mute. The nun leaned closer to Katherine and pointed, with a trembling hand, to the inside of her mouth.

Katherine almost fell from her stool from the shock. She gasped. Were it not for the nun's hand on her arm stabilising her, she would've knocked over the basin of water.

Half of the poor woman's tongue had been cut off. It looked like it had been severed with a blunt, serrated object, causing a jagged blackened stub to remain in its place. It had been cut right down to the very muscle, which would explain why the woman couldn't speak. She hadn't been born a mute; she had been robbed of her ability to speak by Sister Nora in an inhumane, violent manner.

Katherine had to look away from the grotesque sight for a few moments. When she tried to speak, Sister Sorcha once again raised her finger to her lips, reminding her to keep quiet. She pulled a few scraps of paper from her habit, fumbling with them as she rearranged their order, before thrusting them into Katherine's hands. Katherine glanced down at the paper, now crumpled in her hands. The nun nodded in encouragement and beckoned her to read the papers.

Katherine let out a nervous breath and was just about to read the first slip when a booming voice interrupted her from behind.

'I warned you! I warned both of you!' Sister Nora barked in an icy tone.

The sound of the running water had masked any outside noise, so Katherine and Sister Sorcha had not heard her enter the room. Sister Sorcha's eyes widened and darted towards the slips of paper in Katherine's hands.

Katherine thought Sister Nora hadn't seen what was in her hands yet. She quickly crumpled them up further into a ball and dropped it at her feet. She stood up and discretely kicked the ball away from them, eager to keep the contents hidden from Sister Nora's eagle eyes.

Sister Sorcha moved towards Sister Nora, head bowed in submission and fear. Sister Nora raised her left hand, demanding that the frail nun remain still.

Sister Nora directed her chilling words only to Katherine. 'You stupid little girl. Have I not been clear, time and time again, that your meddlesome ways have consequences? You aren't deserving of having any so-called friends within these walls. You are an evil, insolent child and will continue to be treated as such for as long as I am here. You would think, considering how many times your hands have been cut open, that you would learn to heed my warnings. Perhaps I was wrong; you're clearly too stupid for the message to sink in. I will have to greatly increase my efforts to ensure I won't have to repeat this message again. But what to do with you?'

Katherine's eyes skittered to Sister Sorcha, instinctually. She hadn't meant to look in her direction, and Sister Nora noticed. She leaned in towards Katherine, tilted her head back and let out a raucous laugh. Katherine and Sister Sorcha glanced at each other with caution, their whole bodies trembling. They didn't know what Sister Nora was finding so funny, but they both knew that they were better off not knowing and chose to remain silent. Sister Nora snapped her head back up and turned on her heel as if to walk away. She clutched the crucifix with one hand while waving a finger between the two of them, as if having difficulty choosing between the two. Finally, her finger stood still in front of Sister Sorcha. She dropped her hand and rolled her eyes, as though bored by the whole situation, but at the last minute, she turned to face Katherine and smirked. Her face twisted so much, it was almost unrecognisable. She was morphing into a distorted, dark form in front of her. A shroud of darkness descended upon the room as Sister Nora's back became rigid, as if being held up by an unseen force.

Sister Sorcha's breathing has started to come in short gasps as she looked on with wide, fearful eyes. She dropped her shaking hands which had been clasped together in the form of hurried prayer and dropped her head down further. Katherine wanted to move, but something was stopping her. She was frozen to the ground. She wanted to reach out to Sorcha, but her body was no longer obeying her. The frail nun raised her head to sneak a glance at Katherine. There were pools of unshed tears in her eyes, but even then she managed to offer the orphan a weak attempt at a comforting smile.

Katherine allowed herself to smile back at her, even though she knew Sister Nora was observing their every action. But it didn't matter now. It was too late to protect Sorcha, so there was no need to hide their friendship. The fact that Sister Sorcha was able to smile through her stilling fear gave Katherine a smidge of optimism. She looked over at Sister Nora and, in an instant, that optimism died. The nun was staring right back at her with cold, dead eyes and her arms folded across her body. She smiled at Katherine so tightly, her upper lip receded back into her gums.

Sister Nora carelessly grabbed Sorcha by the arm and pushed her towards the door, causing the nun to stumble on her way. From where she was standing, Katherine could tell the elderly woman was sobbing, her shoulders shuddering up and down as each sob racked its way through her body. Sister Sorcha didn't look back once. Katherine knew deep down this would be the last time she would see her.

Sister Nora gave Katherine one last smirk as she followed Sister Sorcha, slamming the door shut behind them.

XVIII

A few minutes later when Katherine found the courage to move again, she ran to the window to see if she could spot them, but both nuns were long gone. She couldn't even make out their footsteps in the gravel. All that was outside were deep puddles of muddy water. Katherine raised her hand to the glass in despair and let it rest there for a few moments, willing with all her might, if there was a God, that he would hear her pleas to save Sister Sorcha. She bit down on her fist to try to quieten the sobs that wouldn't cease. Her breathing had become so ragged, the window she was leaning on began to fog up. She could only see blurred shapes now when she looked outside.

She sniffed and used her apron to wipe her nose. She looked around the room in despair. What was she to do now? Was she to just carry on as if something horrific wasn't happening to Sister Sorcha right now? Just go back to her chores? The pile of laundry she'd been tackling was long forgotten, and the water was now stone-cold. She moved over to the taps to turn them off before the sinks were overfilled. She looked up to the heavens, searching for answers. She had once again tried to do right, both by Sorcha and herself, and in every possible way had failed.

She didn't know what was going to happen to Sister Sorcha, but it was clear that there was very little that Sister Nora was unwilling to do. The very thought made her fearful, and her hands started to feel clammy.

As she returned to her work, Katherine trod on something soft. She peered down.

Sister Sorcha's notes!

Still sniffling, Katherine bent down to retrieve the ball of papers and sank down on her stool to unfold them. After scanning her eyes over the first few words, she soon realised that Sister Sorcha had been trying to convey her story to Katherine; why she had been so afraid of Sister Nora and how she ended up with her tongue as it was. Katherine struggled to figure out which piece of paper she was meant to start with as some of the sentences were difficult to decipher. Sister Sorcha's handwriting was more of an awkward cursive scrawl rather than actual writing, so Katherine had to hold the pieces of paper up to the light to try to distinguish the words.

I knew what she was doing. I stumbled across her one evening two summers ago. I was up in the gallery saying the rosary before my nightly duties when I heard a commotion down below. It frightened me at first, so I ducked down and hid by the pew, but as the noises got more aggressive, I slipped down towards the front so I was able to see what was happening while still being safely hidden from whoever was down there. It was cowardly of me to hide, and I know that God will punish me for that when my time comes, but judging by what I saw next, God has bigger problems protecting those in the orphanage than he does with making me attest to my cowardice.

There was a young girl who had only just come to us; a real slip of a girl who was trying to swing her fists at Sister Nora, but it was an extremely unfair fight because the girl was so weak. I'm not sure how it started, but it was chaotic. Pews had toppled over, and the young girl was trying to crawl away. She was completely covered in blood, whereas Nora was unscathed by their altercation. Her habit wasn't even tousled. Sister Nora was like a vicious animal. She stalked after the girl like an African lion hunting its prey, and when she managed to reach her on the altar steps, she slashed at and bashed the girl until she went limp. I must have made a startled noise from the gallery because the next thing I knew, everything went quiet, and Sister Nora was standing over me. I don't even know how she managed to get up there so fast. She was like a phantom. Her eyes were wide and unyielding, and she had this calculated yet manic expression on her face. It wasn't human.

I've always believed in the existence of the Devil, but I had never once thought that the Devil would walk among us here in this consecrated place, destroying everything we hold sacred.

I didn't know what to do, so I raised my own crucifix and began to pray, but Sister Nora only laughed at me … she cut out my tongue to stop me from ever speaking of it. Truth be told, I probably wouldn't have spoken about it even if I could. If she had done that to a defenceless little child, then God only knows what she would do to me if I were to speak out against her atrocities. She still has it … my tongue. She keeps it in the old custodia that she has on the shelf in her office. It's just a shrivelled piece of flesh now, but every now and then she calls me in to look at it, to remind me of what will happen if I go against her.

That's why I'm so afraid of her. She isn't a she like you and I; she is something dark and savage. She is the Devil reincarnate,

I am sure of it, and that crucifix of hers, the curse of the original sin it bears, it gives her a power beyond any other.

Katherine didn't know why she was surprised by what she had read. She had seen the contents of Father Michael's journals and experienced the sadistic side of Sister Nora herself, but reading Sister Sorcha's story somehow felt different. It was easy for her to distance herself from the gory details within the journals because she had never met the girl. However, reading the details of Sorcha's desperate tale and realising the extent of her fear tugged at Katherine's heartstrings; she found it impossible to distance herself anymore. Once again, she started to blame herself for having failed to protect the nun from Nora's wrath, especially after the agony she had already experienced.

She had made the vital error of letting her guard down, and Sister Sorcha would ultimately pay the price. Katherine's jaw tightened as she clenched her fists. *How could I have been so stupid?* she thought. Katherine started to pace the room, her movements growing more agitated as the reality of the heart-wrenching situation sank in. Her only friend was gone. She hoped that Sister Nora would make it quick, that she wouldn't prolong the anguish for Sister Sorcha. She didn't deserve to be subjected to pain on her account.

Katherine let the slips of paper fall from her hands into the basin of water as the bubbles consumed them, destroying the horrific words and her first real glimpse into Sister Sorcha's life in the process. *Sister Nora will pay for this*, she thought. *I don't know how, but she will answer to me for this!*

XIX

No one mentioned the fact that Sister Sorcha never returned. Her usual seat in the dining hall was quick to be disposed of, making it look like she had never even sat there, not that anyone even appeared to notice its absence.

Katherine was walking the grounds later that evening, trying to pass the time before she had to go to evening mass, when she passed the rickety fence surrounding the new grave-yard. She'd never had a reason to go inside the fence before, but now she felt drawn to do so. Every nerve in her body was screaming at her to venture inside. Taking great care, she opened the gate, the metal creaking as she did so, and made her way inside. She was careful to walk along the edge of the worn path just in case she stepped upon any of the unmarked graves by accident. She reached a row of roughly dug mounds of earth that were in varying stages of regrowth. Some had grass starting to resprout, while others were still piles of mud and stone. She stopped in front of a lone mound at the end, which she thought was the most recent. A shovel lay only a few inches away from the unearthed mud. It looked like someone had tried to compact the earth, concealing what was hidden underneath. Katherine knew she had been drawn to this spot for a reason.

This had to be Sister Sorcha; she knew it without needing to give the ground a second glance. She was about to kneel, to pay her respects to her fallen friend, when the hairs on the back of her neck shot up. Someone was watching her. She could feel their eyes observing her every movement, analysing her reaction to discovering the grave. Sister Sorcha's horrific and untimely disappearance had made her even more wary of Sister Nora. She had a sickening feeling the nun would soon grow tired of her sadistic mind games and horrific physical torment.

She turned on her heel, slipping on some of the lumps of mud in the process, and looked around to see if she could catch Sister Nora watching her. There was no one, but before turning back to the grave, she glimpsed a mysterious figure through an upstairs window. She hadn't been quick enough to catch who it was but, as she only had enemies within these walls, it could have been anyone. She took a deep breath and knelt next to the grave. Sister Nora surely couldn't stop her from saying her final goodbye. She made a mental note to pick some of the daisies that were growing by the hedge to place them on the grave. She recognised this was silly, whimsical, and frankly a little childish, and that there was a chance someone would notice the flowers and throw them away, but she felt she owed it to Sorcha to try to leave something positive on her final resting place.

She noticed a light grey, roundish stone had been placed at the top of the mound, which, she presumed, was the head of the grave. Wanting to keep the grave as natural and undis-turbed as she could, she decided to remove it. She was about to toss it over the fence when she noticed some strange markings on the back of it. They were difficult to make out clearly due to the caked-on mud, but they seemed to be a group of circles, reminding her of coins. She knew she had seen the markings somewhere before but couldn't put her finger on where. She placed the stone inside her pocket, wiped her hands on her dress and went back inside the orphanage. She would have to figure out later why those markings were so familiar and what the meaning was behind them.

Later that night, after Sister Nora had done her rounds through the girls' dormitory, Katherine leaned over the side of her bed and reached for the dress that she had worn earlier that day. She pulled out the stone and held it towards the little sliver of light that was coming through the window. Thankfully, there was a full moon outside, so she didn't have to strain her eyes too much to see the markings. She cleaned the excess mud from it using a rag that she had stolen from the kitchen during clean up earlier that evening. She stared at the stone for a few moments, twisting it around in her hand, trying to work out where she had seen the markings before. Startingly, she recalled a conversation she'd had with Father Michael a few weeks ago. *No wonder it's so familiar*, Katherine thought. His words echoed in her head, clear as day, 'Judas received thirty pieces of silver'. Of course, it all made sense to her now; she had seen the same markings on one of the worn tapestries downstairs.

She couldn't believe it had taken her so long to make the connection. There were tapestries placed all around the orphanage and each of them had a symbol on it to denote each disciple. But why, out of all the symbols to place on a nun's grave, would there be a representation of Judas? And who would have put it there? It just didn't make sense to her.

She lowered her head in defeat, disappointed with herself for not being able to figure everything out and being left with more questions than answers yet again. She used her two index fingers to rub her temples. Her head was hurting from all the confusion. She sat, staring blankly into space for a few moments, before deciding, with great reluctance, that she needed to investigate further and find out why the stone was placed on Sister Sorcha's grave. She owed her that much, at least.

Katherine spent a few seconds weighing up her options. The image of Sister Nora kept intruding into her mind like an omen. She was already on thin ice with the madwoman, and she didn't want to give her any ammunition to hurt her again. But then, what did she have to lose? She was punished even when she'd done nothing wrong! So, shouldn't she at least try to pursue the answers to her questions? She would just have to be extremely careful how she went about it.

XX

Sister Nora had already locked the doors in the dormitory when she had done her rounds earlier that evening, so the only way Katherine could get out was by picking the lock to her bedroom. She had broken into her father's cabinet a few times as a child. He'd kept his winnings from betting on horses in it. Unfortunately for him, he was always too drunk to count the money he'd won, so he never noticed when a few pounds went missing here and there.

She pursed her lips together in concentration and looked around the room, searching for something sharp enough to act as a lockpick. Nothing would suffice, so she turned her attention to her bed. The base was ancient and rusting with age. She thought it must've been there since the orphanage first opened. Maintenance wasn't exactly a top priority for Sister Nora, who preferred a threadbare, impoverished aesthetic for the orphanage. Katherine pushed her mattress to the side and, using all her might, tugged one of the wires until she heard the sharp 'ping' of it coming loose.

It was quite long, but she had no other options, so it would have to do. She would have to hide the wire under her bed when she was finished if she wasn't able to force it back into place. She tiptoed stealthily over to her door and placed the wire into the lock with exact precision. She leaned down with her ear next to the lock. It took a few minutes of wiggling the wire around before she heard the lock snap open. A weight released from her chest as she wiped her sweaty hands on her nightdress. She hadn't remembered it being that stressful when she was picking the lock back home.

She was wary as she placed the wire by the door, careful not to make any noise, and stepped up to the threshold, her heart racing with each movement, the weight of exhaustion pressing down on her shoulders. She peered outside, making sure that no prying eyes were about before bravely stepping out into the hallway, which was notorious for its creaky floorboards. She would have to stay right next to the walls to try to avoid them. She edged along the dark hallway, her back flush against the cold, damp walls, and made her way to the nuns' quarters. She wasn't sure what she was looking for exactly, but decided Sister Sorcha's room would be the best place to start. She just hoped it would be unlocked. Otherwise, she would be stuck without any options.

She knew the nuns had their own individual rooms, so at least she wouldn't have to contend with running into any 'roommates'. It was lucky, too, that each room had the nun's name engraved on a wooden plate next to their door, otherwise she could have easily slipped into the wrong room. Her stomach dropped at the very thought. What if she had walked right into Sister Nora's room? That would be the end of her; there would be no coming back from that. She shook the frightening thought from her head and continued making her way down the hall, searching for Sister Sorcha's room. After a while, she came to one door which was missing a nameplate. *This must be her room,* she thought. She placed her hand tentatively on the doorknob. Her hands were shaking, either from apprehension or the cold, Katherine wasn't quite sure, but she managed to turn the knob with minimal noise. *Thank God it's not locked*, she thought. She made her way inside, shutting the door behind her.

Sister Sorcha's room was exactly as she had expected it to be. It was similar to hers, containing a single bed with thread-bare linen. A wooden crucifix was nailed above the head of the bed, and there was a small writing desk in the corner with a half-melted candle and a string of rosary beads lying in a neat pile next to it. There were two little windows which were so narrow they were more like slits and allowed little light into the room. The whole room had a heavy smell of sage. Katherine spotted a little box of matches beside the candle and decided to make use of what was left of the candle stump. She struck a match, and the flickering flame gave her enough light to see every detail in the room.

There were very few personal items in the room and no letters or notes left in the drawer of her desk. The only thing Katherine recognised as Sorcha's was a string of rosary beads on the desk. She had seen her take them from her pocket on more than one occasion. The stark reality hit Katherine, just how quickly a person can be gone. She took a deep breath. The familiar smell of Sister Sorcha hit her in the face like a wave and her eyes started watering. She ran her hands over the rosary beads nervously, almost afraid to touch the only thing left of her friend. In her anxious state, she dropped the beads, and they clattered to the floor.

'Oh, for God's sake,' Katherine huffed as she paused her movements. She held her breath as she waited to make sure no one had heard her.

The flame from the candle suddenly went out, and she was encased in total darkness. When no one appeared, she got onto her hands and knees and started feeling around for the beads. She managed to feel her way over to the bed and braced herself up on one hand while she leaned underneath to find the beads. She edged her hand underneath and patted it around trying to feel for them. Instead of finding the beads, she felt multiple grooves on the floorboards. They were too deep and rough for them not to have been made deliberately, and they were splintering slightly. She scrambled back to the desk where she found another match and relit the candle. She brought the candle over to the bed, moved Sorcha's mattress over to one side and kneeled back on the floor to have a better look at the carvings.

Katherine's breath hitched in surprise. The same markings she'd found on the stone were carved deep into the floor.

XXI

Katherine sat back on her haunches and pondered this bizarre occurrence. It seemed so strange to her, and she just couldn't see any reason as to why this symbol would be following Sister Sorcha. What did it mean? And what did the markings have to do with Sister Sorcha? Perhaps, she hadn't even been aware they were there. Why would someone try to connect the kindly nun with someone as immoral as Judas? But then again, Katherine hadn't known her that well. Other than the torture she endured at the hands of Sister Nora and the caring personality that she showed her, Katherine really knew very little of the type of person her comrade was when she wasn't around. Could there have been another side to her that she was careful to keep hidden? Anything was possible, but Katherine was reluctant to believe badly of the nun who had been her only support. There must be another explanation.

She snuffed out what was left of the candle, forgoing any more attempts at retrieving the rosary beads, placed the little stub of wax back on the desk, and skirted her way over to the door. She waited a few moments before proceeding to open the door, straining her ears for the sound of anyone walking in the hallway before pulling the door closed behind her. Once she was certain that the coast was clear, she inched out into the hall and sprinted along the edge of the wall once again, back to the safety of her own dorm room.

That part of the corridor seemed too dark and desolate. There was a faint glow of light coming from underneath the doors of the other nuns; most of them were still awake, saying their final prayers for the night, so their candles were still alight. She could hear the low murmur of methodical prayer if she really strained her ears. Sister Sorcha's room stood out like an ominous presence amongst the others, a reminder of the heavy existence of death within the walls. There was complete darkness even in the areas surrounding her room, and it sent shivers down Katherine's spine.

She shuffled into her room and used the wire to lock the door again. She needed everything to look exactly as it was when Sister Nora had done her rounds earlier that night. She shuddered as she imagined Sister Nora's wrath if she found Katherine's door unlocked. The results would be catastrophic.

She tiptoed over to her bed and moved the mattress back again. It would be better to replace the wire rather than try to dispose of it. But despite her vigorous efforts, it kept slipping out of place. She had no choice but to stash it somewhere. But where? There weren't many hiding spaces at her disposal. Hiding it underneath her bed was less than ideal – too easy for someone to find it. However, she didn't have any other options. She sighed and knelt down, then inched the wire as far back into the bed frame as possible. As she retracted her hand, she paused. The floorboards felt bumpy, just as Sister Sorcha's had been, as though they'd been gouged with something sharp.

She hauled the bedframe to one side to get a better view of what was there. Katherine had a sinking feeling in her stomach, knowing deep down what was carved into her floor, but she needed to see it with her own eyes. The pattern of strange coincidences that had emerged recently could lead to only one explanation. With blustering hands, she jumped up and grabbed a nearby candle and had to strike a match a few times to be able to set the wick alight. She knelt again with caution and brought the candle right up next to where she had felt the carvings. Her breath started to come in short bursts and the bile rose in her throat as the etching became clear. Father Michael had been right from the start; Sister Nora had been watching her. Marking her. Targeting her.

Katherine raised her hand to her mouth to stop herself from screaming. Right under her bed were the markings of the thirty pieces of silver of Judas. They were dotted across the large space as if the coins had been tossed there. Her shaking hands were causing the candle flame to flicker, sending the etching into the dark abyss and back again. The symbol of Judas' sin was directly under where she laid her head every night. She was being tarred with the same brush as Judas.

Katherine knew she wasn't perfect, that some of her actions had made her mother think there was a darkness hidden within her, especially after the incidents with Michelle and the imbecile Seamus all those years ago. Katherine still couldn't see, however, why her mother had an issue with it. It wasn't that she was evil; she'd had a good reason. All she had done was eliminate a problem that was making her own life unbearable. She was looking after herself because no one else would. Was that the reason for the markings? Did Sister Nora know about what she'd done to Michelle and Seamus, and was she making it her mission to punish her for her supposed wrongdoings? But that still didn't explain why Sorcha had been targeted as well. What did Sister Nora know about Sorcha? Had she done something in her past life that Sister Nora deemed to be worthy of punishment? Or had her 'wrongdoing' simply been allowing a friendship to blossom in an environment that bred only darkness and despair?

All the fear and apprehension that Katherine had succumbed to in the last few months vanished in an instant. Those emotions lifted from her body like a veil and were replaced with outrage. The anger that coursed through her veins was like a raging fire bubbling inside her. How dare Sister Nora play God and punish her for what she'd done. That boy was a burden to everyone around him; she'd merely done a service for her parish and herself, and she refused to feel sorry for it. He got what he deserved. As for Michelle, well, she was just too weak to justify her existence. If there was one teaching from the Bible that Katherine remembered well, it was when God had said, 'An eye for an eye'. *If it was in the Bible, it couldn't be wrong … could it?* She stood up and began to pace the room, muttering in anger. She was so furious she could have punched the wall out of frustration.

What a hypocrite Sister Nora was! After every sordid sin she'd committed against innocent people for decades. Katherine didn't care if it was the crucifix making her do it. Whatever Sister Sorcha had done would never match up to the atrocities Sister Nora had committed herself. Katherine scoffed in disbelief and blew out her candle, almost spitting at it in her haste. She pulled her bed and mattress back into its original place and lay down to go to sleep. Lying on her back, staring blankly at the ceiling for what felt like hours, her anger continued swirling in the pit of her stomach, making it impossible for her to doze off. She kept reliving the events that had occurred in the orphanage since she'd been brought there.

Every agonising stroke of pain, all the abuse and the isolation she'd felt was because Sister Nora had taken it upon herself to act as judge, jury and executioner. A woman so obsessed with a gaudy crucifix – no … controlled by it – had tormented Katherine for something she'd committed years ago.

Katherine rolled over and hit her pillow in frustration. She hated Sister Nora, hated the enormity of her power over her helpless victims. She vowed she wouldn't be afraid of her any longer. She wouldn't hide herself for fear of the extreme repercussions. Not anymore. She couldn't believe how stupid she had been, allowing Sister Nora to make her a pawn of the Devil. She shook her head and smirked. She vowed that, one way or another, she would find a way to have revenge on Sister Nora, not just for herself, but for the rest of the orphans, and Sister Sorcha too.

If Sister Nora thought Katherine was evil, then she would show her just how evil she could be. She would have to come up with a foolproof plan, but her mind was racing with possibilities. Sister Nora was cunning; Katherine would have to remain quiet and subdued in case she aroused any suspicion. With her newfound perspective and the titillating taste of revenge to come, Katherine's eyes finally grew heavy with sleep. She drifted off as the heavy vibrations of the organ being played lulled her to sleep.

XXII

The following week, Katherine sat alone in the graveyard next to Sister Sorcha's plot. She just couldn't fathom it. She guessed that in Sister Nora's twisted mind, she thought her persecution of Sorcha was justified. So, what did she know about Sister Sorcha? Was she hiding a secret from her past too? But what sordid mystery would she have concealed?

It was sheer curiosity at this point that made Katherine want to know the answer to her question, but she had no resources to help her find out. Perhaps she just had to accept the fact that some questions would never be answered here.

Katherine was just beginning to resign herself to this fact when she heard an awkward cough behind her. Startled by the noise, she jumped and whipped her head around to face the intruder. Father Michael was standing right outside the graveyard fence. He appeared nervous as he twisted his cap between his hands and refused to meet her eye. He gestured towards the graveyard with a limp hand, silently asking Katherine for permission to enter the grounds.

Suspicious of his actions, Katherine narrowed her eyes and, with reluctance, nodded her head, allowing him to join her next to Sister Sorcha's grave.

It was silent for a few moments before Father Michael broke the peace by speaking. 'She wasn't what you thought she was,' he said matter-of-factly.

Not wanting to hear any falsities about her friend, Katherine stood up to face him as her anger poured out. 'You didn't even know her!' she shouted. She couldn't believe the audacity of Father Michael.

He sighed. 'You're right. I didn't exactly know her. But I know what I saw, and she was quite … light fingered.'

Katherine scoffed in disbelief and folded her arms across her chest.

'I know you don't believe it, but before you came here there were many cases of orphans' personal possessions going missing. Of course, finding the items wasn't on Sister Nora's radar so they were never recovered. There was chatter in the halls and some of the girls began to turn on each other, but no one knew who the culprit was. That was until Sister Sorcha was with me in the chapel one evening. She always offered to clean up after the sermons after everyone had retired to bed. It just so happened that I had a few things that I had forgotten to attend to, so I arrived later than planned that night. I think perhaps she didn't hear me entering the chapel as she had her back to me when I arrived. At first, I took no notice of what she was doing, but then I saw her about to slip a small chalice into her pocket. I called out to her, and she dropped it in fright. I moved towards her, and we both bent down to pick it up. I heard a metallic sound coming from her pocket, like small chains rattling together. Our eyes met, and she blushed. I asked her to empty her pockets, but she refused, so I reached into her pocket and pulled out some of the necklaces that had been stolen from the girls that week.

'I couldn't believe it; she was the last person I would have thought would steal from anyone. Like you, I had been misled believing she was an honest, gentle soul, but alas,' said Father Michael before clearing his throat, 'looks can be deceiving.'

'I was firm with her … told her she needed to return all the items she had taken, and I thought that would be the end of it. She shuffled down the chapel aisle, off towards the double doors and, just when she thought I wasn't looking, she pocketed something else on her way out. She couldn't help herself; it was habitual. The necklaces were never returned. Items still went missing, but the incidents weren't as frequent as they had been. Every time there were whisperings about trying to find the possessions that had been taken, Sister Sorcha would make herself scarce. She never stopped that little habit.'

Stumped by the tales of her thieving friend, Katherine slumped back onto the ground, lost for words. She didn't want to believe it. Father Michael had no reason to lie to her now, though, so maybe she hadn't known Sister Sorcha as well as she thought she had.

'There are always two sides to everyone, Katherine. You should know this better than anyone. Some people are just very good at keeping the more sinful side hidden from the world. Eventually, it gets harder for them to keep the darkness buried in a box. It starts to creep out in waves, and people see glimpses of it. At first, they aren't quite sure if they believe what they see, because the person is different from the one they knew. It takes them a while to realise it was all an elaborate façade. A ruse to hide that person's flawed self.'

Katherine remained quiet as she absorbed what Father Michael had said. She understood his profound observation and knew it to be true. She had always believed that some of the village girls were putting on an act; they were just too good to be true. No one is that pure. She nodded her head, more to herself than in agreement with Father Michael, and looked up at him from underneath her eyelashes.

His piercing stare hinted there was another meaning behind his words. 'I've been told that this particular concept may speak deeply to you and your own habits,' he murmured.

Katherine gritted her teeth and narrowed her eyes into menacing slits. *What does he know?* she thought as she clenched her fists, but Father Michael seemed undeterred by her obvious anger towards him. He clicked his tongue and strode off to the chapel with his hands clasped firmly behind his back. To the innocent bystander, he appeared very much a man at ease.

As soon as he was out of sight, Katherine allowed herself to relax and unclenched her fists. Her nails had left sharp indentations on her palm. She closed her eyes out of frustration and tutted to herself.

Father Michael didn't know her on a personal level and, other than his sinister confessions to her a few months prior, she hadn't told him anything that would warrant that level of judgement. It wasn't possible that he knew what she had done. Sister Nora must have told him. It was evident he was more than a mere henchman for Sister Nora. She wouldn't have shared such secrets with anyone of such lowly status. No, their relationship was much more personal than he'd admitted.

The irony of it all wasn't lost on Katherine. What a hypocrite – highlighting his belief that everyone has two sides, as if he were somehow exempt. There wasn't one living person in the orphanage that this didn't apply to. Katherine had seen it all around her and hadn't thought twice about it. It was just a way of life for those living in the Convent of Mercy. Fear drove the girls to do terrible things and hide their actions, then in return, they let the darkness hidden deep within them emerge to the surface.

No wonder the crucifix has so much power over Sister Nora, Katherine thought.

The walls are steeped with sin.

XXIII

Katherine was becoming a woman possessed. She spent every waking minute plotting how she would get back at Sister Nora – what it would feel like, the look on Sister Nora's face – but every time she thought of a possibility, it didn't feel right to her. She wanted her revenge to be monumental. She wanted Sister Nora to pay for the full extent of what she had done. She noticed the darkness beginning to ascend within her, but she convinced herself that it and her calculating thoughts were normal. That she was in complete control of herself.

However, this couldn't have been further from the truth. Her thoughts were consuming her. She had lost a noticeable amount of weight, and there were dark, heavy bags beginning to form underneath her eyes. Had she been close to anyone in the orphanage, it would have been cause for concern, but her isolation meant that these changes went undetected.

She lurked around the corners of hallways, hidden in the shadows, and watched every one of Sister Nora's movements. She needed to know if she had a weakness that could be exploited, and studied her daily patterns.

One evening, as the sun was beginning to set, the orphans made their way to the dining hall for their evening meal. They pushed each other in their eagerness to get to the dining room for their next meagre meal. By contrast, Katherine took her time. She didn't feel hunger anymore and was too caught up in her own thoughts to pay attention to what was going on around her. Sinking down into her seat, she toyed with her spoon while she watched the door in anticipation of the nuns' usual procession.

All of a sudden, one of the girls sitting next to her grabbed her wrist, forcing her hand to remain still. Katherine turned to glare at her, confused by the girl's behaviour. She was met by a pair of wide, doe-like eyes and a quivering chin.

'Please stop,' she whispered. 'What are you doing? You're going to get in trouble if someone sees what you're doing,' she said as she nodded in the direction of the table.

Katherine looked down and understood why she had been so concerned. She'd been so focused on watching the door that, without realising it, she had been digging the spoon into the table, marking it in the process. She dropped the spoon, straightened her back and relaxed her hands, aware that her actions had frightened the girl.

'I'm so sorry … I didn't realise what I was doing. It won't happen again,' she said and gave her a fleeting smile.

The young girl glanced at Katherine nervously before turning away.

Katherine exhaled as a wave of calm washed over her and rolled her neck to reduce some tension. She noticed how badly she had damaged the table. The varnish was scratched off and the wood had been chipped.

She swallowed her frustration. *So much for remaining subtle*, Katherine thought, rolling her eyes. She turned to look back at the door once again, just as the bell rang to signal the entrance of the nuns.

The dining hall fell silent as the girls focused their attention on their plates. Nobody dared to look up, except for Katherine. She wanted to look Sister Nora in the eye as her first act of sheer defiance. She wanted to show her she was no longer afraid of her and refused to be submissive. The nuns made their way towards their seats, in a moving wave of black and white, with Sister Nora taking up her usual place at the back of the row. Katherine clenched her hands. She couldn't help the anger stirring in her stomach and started to shake with rage.

As if sensing a shift in the girls' mood, Sister Nora scanned the room until her eyes came to rest on Katherine, her malevolent smirk fading as they locked eyes. Her brow was furrowed, and her eyes were narrowed into slits. Katherine took the nun's confused expression as a personal victory and refused to break eye contact as Sister Nora took her seat at the top table. As Katherine had expected, Sister Nora reached up to clutch the crucifix around her neck as if trying to absorb strength from it. It was clear she didn't know what to do about Katherine's defiance … *and* that she didn't like it.

The bell dinged once again and everyone tucked into their food, bar Sister Nora. Katherine sneaked a glance at the top table every now and then and noticed that Sister Nora hadn't stopped looking at her. Her plate remained untouched. Katherine placed her cutlery down once more and, in yet another act of defiance, leaned forward to give Sister Nora a smirk of her own. The nun's face turned dark as the madness returned like a shrouded veil.

Unexpectedly, the doors burst open, breaking the tension between Katherine and Sister Nora and shattering the silence. In stomped a mangey-looking girl, wearing a tattered short sleeved frock. Katherine couldn't recollect ever seeing her before. Some of the younger orphans, shocked by the brazen outburst, had dropped their cutlery in fear. One girl knocked over her water glass, resulting in a mess of shattered glass and water all over the table. Shocked and terrified that they'd be punished for having disrupted the silence themselves, some of them began to sob.

The young girl who burst into the dining room marched past the orphans, shouting obscenities as she went.

'You're a monster!' she shouted. 'An evil woman that even God won't be able to save!'

Sister Nora abruptly stood up but didn't utter a word. Instead, to Katherine's surprise, she let the girl continue her brazen tirade. Katherine, unbothered by what was happening, scrutinised the girl in the middle of the room. She was quite young, around eleven or twelve years old. Her hair was greasy and matted. She was limping and clutching one of her arms close to her chest. Her ashen face was stained from tears and her lips were split and quivering uncontrollably.

Katherine leaned forward and could see that the arm she was holding was discoloured and bent in an odd shape. Katherine clicked her tongue and nodded her head in under-standing. This girl had been sent to Sister Nora's office earlier, and this was the unfortunate result of the 'meeting'.

Katherine turned her gaze to Sister Nora, trying gauge how she felt about this extraordinary outburst. She had a scowl that could darken the skies. Her hands were gripping her glass of wine so tightly, Katherine thought it would shatter from the pressure. The girl's outburst wouldn't go unpunished, Katherine surmised. Most likely, this would be the first and last time that Katherine would see this damaged girl.

Katherine was numb to the inevitability of her death. It had become a part of her life now and it no longer shocked her.

The quivering girl started to walk towards the head table, her shrill screams echoing throughout the hall as she shouted at Sister Nora. However, she didn't have a chance to get there as Sister Nora had already moved towards her, knocking some of the plates over in the process. The sound of the porcelain hitting the floor and shattering into pieces didn't register with Sister Nora as she was focused solely on stopping the girl in her tracks. She flew towards the orphan, sending plates tumbling to the floor in her fury, and her heels clacked against the floor with every forceful step towards the unfortunate orphan. She grasped the young girl's neck, lifting her off her feet and putting an immediate stop to her manic screaming.

This was the first time Katherine had seen Sister Nora carry out an abusive act in public. Usually, she waited until the darkest part of the night, when everyone was sleeping.

Katherine looked around the room, observing everyone's emotions, like a spectator watching a dramatic show. Some of the orphans began screaming hysterically, while others were frozen to their seats, trembling with trepidation. Some clutched each other, their faces red and swollen from the endless tears streaming down. She thought one of the girls was vomiting because she heard retching sounds from one of the tables.

The nuns, who had never once lifted their heads at dinner and were always so submissive, were standing up, frozen, eyes wide with fear. Some raised their rosary beads in an act of deep faith, hoping the force of their prayers would make Sister Nora stop her horrific actions, while others kept glancing at the doors, perhaps considering leaving the room.

Sister Nora tightened her grip on the young girl, her face twisting in determination. She used her other hand to force the girl backwards, causing her to trip and fall. The girl tried to crawl away from her, but the nun was relentless in her pursuit. Sister Nora bent down and dragged the girl up by her hair, pulling her from the room. The girl begged her to stop, kicking and shrieking as she attempted to get away. She managed to get a grip with her good hand on the doorframe on the way out, but Sister Nora pried her fingers loose, breaking her grip. The door banged shut behind them as they disappeared down the hallway, out of sight of the rest of the witnesses.

Katherine could still hear the shrill screams and pleas for mercy but couldn't hear any verbal response from Nora, only an incessant thumping sound as she presumably hit the girl. The sounds gradually faded away and the orphans' sobbing had ceased as they slowly regained control of themselves. Silence reigned once more as the sharp clang of metal hitting the floor resounded in the room

Katherine listened intently as she heard a door being opened and heavy footsteps. Sister Nora was speaking to whoever had entered – a man, judging by the low timbre of his replies. Then, there was the unmistakable sound of something heavy being dragged across the floorboards. Katherine presumed Father Michael had been told to dispose of the body.

Sister Nora returned to the dining hall, her face stoic once more. She showed no signs of dishevelment as she made her way back up the room. The orphans looked at each other in confusion, not knowing what to do. Sister Nora barked at everyone to get back in their seats and they dropped down to the benches, afraid Sister Nora would inflict her remaining wrath on them if they were too slow.

Sister Nora sat in her usual spot at the head table, pushing the broken plates aside before looking around the room with narrowed eyes. It was frightening how quickly she had managed to compose herself. Other than a speck of blood on the collar of her habit, no one would guess she'd just committed a murderous act right outside the door. It was as if it hadn't happened at all. She stretched her arm across one of the nuns, who was frozen in her place, and gently picked up the little brass bell on the table. She gave the bell a firm ring and nodded, demanding everyone to return to their meal.

It was as if a switch had been flicked. Everyone responded by picking up their spoons and lowering their heads as they returned to their evening meals, not once looking up again. Katherine was astonished at how Sister Nora had regained control of the entire room with just a flick of her wrist. Her attitude demanded absolute obedience, and, despite the unmitigated horror of her actions, no one uttered a word or attempted to run away. They were completely bent to her will – her own little pawns that she could do with as she pleased and, because they were so afraid of what she could do to them, no one even considered speaking out against her.

Katherine tilted her head to the side in bewilderment. She wondered what it would be like to have that level of control over people. She had never struggled getting people to do what she wanted when she was growing up, but to be able to control an entire building of people, even though you've been abusing and murdering others, was something quite astonishing. If she had that power, she wouldn't have to bow down to anyone anymore. She would no longer be the underdog in the orphanage.

Katherine's lips curved into a smile as she stared at what was left of her own food. What a thing that would be, to possess the enormity of power that Sister Nora had. Katherine picked up her spoon and went back to eating her food, pondering this fresh perspective, while Sister Nora sat watching everyone like a hawk as she tightened the chain of the crucifix around her neck.

XXIV

It was now March, and Katherine had been obsessing about what it would be like to have Sister Nora's power. It was all she thought about. She had to have it. It didn't matter how many beatings she was subjected to or how many orphans disappeared, because soon she would possess the power to stop it all.

She took her beatings without any objections or scornful looks at Sister Nora. The pain didn't even register anymore. The lashings from the riding crop had begun to feel like miniscule pin-pricks dancing on her body. There was a new air about Katherine; a darkness was awakening within her, giving her a smug confidence.

Once Sister Nora had finished her outbursts of rage, Katherine would stand tall and purposely march out the door as if nothing had happened, determined to stick to her vow of not showing fear in front of the sadistic nun. She had even managed to utter a sarcastic 'thank you, Sister' at the end of her last session. In the past, her 'visits' to Sister Nora's office would have left her in excruciating pain and clutching her wounds for the rest of the week, but now, she didn't feel anything. The look of unmistakable frustration on Sister Nora's face made it all worthwhile. She took pride in the fact that Sister Nora was never fully satisfied at the end of her escapades. She didn't even bother to hide her wounds anymore. She was numb to the searing pain that was coursing through her body. The only thing that mattered was obtaining the crucifix.

Father Michael had noticed subtle changes occurring in Katherine. She was retreating into herself, creating a barrier, distancing herself from what was happening around her. Deep black circles under her eyes indicated she wasn't sleeping much, and he'd noticed how excessively focused she was on Sister Nora's activities. He had caught her one morning sneaking around, trying to peer through the high windows of her office. Normally, no one would go near it voluntarily. When he confronted her, she stuttered a mediocre excuse about needing to return something to Sister Nora. He didn't believe her, and when he didn't respond immediately, her whole demeanour changed. She straightened her shoulders as the expression on her face transformed from shock to complete disdain. She glared at him through narrowed eyes and sneered at him before she strutted off down the hallway, without giving a second glance back in his direction.

With shaking hands, he forced his set of rosary beads from the confines of his pocket and blessed himself. Her actions reminded him of the changes he'd observed in Sister Nora all those years ago, the only difference being that Sister Nora had hidden the changes in her personality until she had obtained the crucifix. If Katherine was displaying the signs of her rising darkness now, what would she be like if she managed to obtain it? There was a sinister side to Katherine, and God help everyone should she have the help of the cursed object.

Father Michael's position in the orphanage had its advantages. It enabled him to watch unfolding events from a safe distance as no one paid any attention to the old priest. He guessed Katherine was actively plotting something.

One day, during his sermon, he noticed her sitting in a pew near the back of the chapel. She wasn't paying the slightest bit of attention to what he was saying. Instead, she was staring right at Sister Nora. He could've sworn he saw her raise her right hand to her chest, just as Sister Nora often did when adjusting her crucifix. His stomach clenched with fear. The darkness was threatening to take hold of Katherine much faster than it had with Sister Nora.

He spent the following few evenings alone in his chamber, with his door locked and barricaded. He didn't feel safe in the orphanage anymore. He contemplated how to approach the troubled girl to discover the extent of the changes. He knew she hated him, and he didn't blame her, not when he turned a blind eye to the abuse she received. But he had to convince her that she must fight the evil force enveloping her soul, otherwise nobody would be safe. He had to at least try to prevent history from repeating itself.

The following day he found the courage to approach Katherine. The sky was dull and overcast, with a howling wind. As Father Michael looked out his window at the sky that was threatening to open, he spotted Katherine sitting cross-legged by the statue of Mary in the front yard. She was on her own and was poking the grass with a twig. He grabbed his hat and coat, blessed himself with holy water and strode off to speak with her.

He approached her with caution, the same way someone might try to approach an injured animal to avoid startling it. She seemed oblivious to the cold weather, even though her hands had turned a startling shade of blue. She didn't look up at him as he approached, but she dropped the twig, so he assumed she had sensed his presence.

He cleared his throat, preparing to speak, when, out of nowhere, Katherine whipped her head around and looked at him through darkened slits for eyes. 'Can I help you with something, Father Michael?' she asked in a tone heavy with sarcasm. The wind was whipping her hair around her face, masking the details of her expression.

Father Michael froze mid-step. He hadn't anticipated this being so awkward. Her directness had startled him, and the words he'd been planning to say disappeared from his mind. He clenched his fists into tight balls to stop the tremors. He didn't want her to see how nervous he was.

Finally, he said, 'My child, you must come inside. The weather out here is—'

'I do not care for your tiresome talks about the weather. Let's not pretend that you now suddenly care for my wellbeing. What is it that you want?' she asked.

'I-I am worried about you,' he stuttered. He knelt beside Katherine, cautious not to get too close as he wasn't sure how she would react to his proximity.

'My dear child, what has happened to you? You are not the same person you were before.'

Katherine scoffed. 'You ask what has happened to me as if you don't know. As if you aren't the cause of some of it. Why are you pretending to care now about what has happened to me?' She yawned. 'Doesn't Sister Nora have more bodies for you to make disappear? Is that what's going on right now, Father? Are you bored?'

Father Michael took a shaky breath and sighed. She was clearly pushing him, trying to get him to retaliate, to distract him from why he was speaking with her. But he refused to play her mind games.

'There is an obvious darkness growing inside you. I have seen you watch and wait for Sister Nora in the darkest recesses of the hallways. Did you think that no one noticed? I do not know what is going through your head, but I urge you to stop before it's too late. I know what you have been through, and words cannot express how sorry I am for all you've been put through,' he said.

'These shifts in your behaviour are what I warned you about; they are the same as what I saw happen to Sister Nora decades ago. The darkness is threatening to take control of you, as it did her. You do not possess the cursed object she holds so close to her, so please don't let this place push you towards darkness. I beg you to resist it. There will be no turning back if you give in to it.'

Katherine pursed her lips, picked up the twig once more and continued shoving it into the grass. She didn't respond to him. He wondered if the wind had prevented her from hearing his pleas.

Leaning closer, Father Michael peered at what she was doing and gasped. She hadn't been playing with the twig at all. Unable to fly, an injured bee was crawling between the blades of the grass seeking refuge, but Katherine was using the twig to prevent it from escaping, trapping it, then toying with it, letting it think it was free for a moment, then blocking it from going any further. She seemed to be enjoying the insect's distress.

'What are you doing? Leave it alone, Katherine. We must not harm any of God's creatures,' implored Father Michael as he tried to take the twig from her hand.

Katherine snatched her hand away. 'Don't touch me!' she shouted.

She threw the twig away and chuckled. 'It's laughable really. You must know what a hypocrite you truly are. You care more for this pitiful bug than you do for the children in the building behind us. I believe, if history is any indication, you've caused more harm to God's creatures than I have. I know you helped Sister Nora a few months ago to destroy all evidence of Jane being here, didn't you? I know her uncle wasn't mistaken. She was here before he came looking for her, wasn't she?'

Father Michael's back straightened as he absorbed her question. He hadn't been expecting her to be so abrupt, and he froze as the guilt came flooding back. He met her eyes for a brief moment and became frightened at the aggression he saw swirling in them. 'I-I had no choice,' he stammered. 'I couldn't help Jane … she was already dead by the time I got to Sister Nora's office. You know well enough that once Sister Nora has her mind set on someone, the outcome is inevitable. Jane was destined to die long before she entered that office. Sister Nora knew her uncle would be coming to look for her, and she couldn't risk the potential of Jane telling him what she'd endured. The only way to keep her secret safe was for Jane to disappear, as if she had never existed.'

'How did you do it, Father? How did you make a girl disappear entirely from the orphanage? All her photographs and records are gone from the admission files. Did you burn them? Or did you just bury all record of her with her lifeless body?'

Father Michael began to explain, but Katherine cut him off by raising her hand. 'There's no point in stammering a false explanation now. Don't pretend to have remorse, when you and I both know that you aren't capable of it. You're only capable of self-preservation. But don't forget, I know who you really are and what you've done. For once, how about telling me honestly how you did it?'

Father Michael sighed. He had no choice but to tell her the truth. 'I wasn't lying when I said Jane was already dead by the time I got there. And that night, I wasn't called to help dispose of her like I usually am. I was in my office, and I knew something bad must have happened because the convent was too quiet. I couldn't even hear the whistling of wind through the hallway. It was bizarre, but my hands started to shake and there was this knot in the pit of my stomach. I was jittery, and the flame of the candle on my desk started to flicker before going out, even though there was no air circulating the room. It was like the convent was creating a shroud of darkness. I took it as a sign that I needed to go to Sister Nora, and I was right. I went up the stairs, careful to be discreet, so as not to alert anyone. I knocked on her door, but when she didn't answer, I pushed my way in. Sister Nora was kneeling in front of a large trunk, struggling to fit a girl's legs into it. I thought it was odd that she had opted to use a trunk; she'd never done so before.'

Katherine raised her eyebrows in confusion. 'Why not, Father? A trunk seems like a good way to hide a body.'

Father Michael bit his lip before saying, 'The bodies don't fit in the trunks.'

Katherine said nothing to this gruesome admission. Her lips drew into a tight line as she contemplated his words, nodding her head and considering what he was truly admitting to. Her lack of interjection told him that he was safe to carry on with his explanation.

'I didn't know it was Jane when I walked in, but as soon as I got closer to the trunk, I saw her face clearly. Of course, I was shocked, but there was nothing I could do at that point.' His chin started to tremble. 'For the sake of the orphanage and Sister Nora, the only option I had was to help make the body disappear.'

Katherine's attention returned to the bee, but Father Michael sensed she was waiting for him to say more. He swallowed a groan of frustration, realising there was no point in hiding the gory details from her.

'We had to break Jane's arms and dislocate her right shoulder to make her fit in the trunk,' he said, shaking his head sadly. 'I haven't been able to get the sound of her little bones snapping from my mind. It took a great amount of effort ...' His words drifted off as he hung his head.

Katherine snapped the twig she'd been holding and tossed it towards the convent, ending Father Michael's stomach-curling story. Startled by the snap, Father Michael glanced up to look at Katherine. He coughed and dusted his hands on his thighs, trying in desperation to distract himself from the swirling storm raging in Katherine's eyes.

He continued softly. 'I don't know how, but Sister Nora knew that Jane's uncle was going to turn up. She never divulges the source of her knowledge to me.' He frowned. 'That's why she hadn't called me earlier. She had to act fast. She was frantic once the deed was done and wouldn't stop pacing around the room, muttering under her breath. I couldn't make out what she was saying as she wasn't speaking in English. It sounded ancient, possibly Latin, but these days my Latin could use a bit of work.' He paused. 'Once I had managed to force the clasp on the trunk closed, I took a better look at Sister Nora.

'She had taken the crucifix from her neck and was clasping it in both her hands. She was holding it so tightly that her palms started to drip blood onto the floorboards. Wisps of her hair had escaped from underneath her habit, and her eyes were black and frenzied, like a shark that had just tasted its first drop of blood. I hadn't seen her this dishevelled before, so it was quite startling. I moved towards her, but she jerked away, snapping out of what I assume was the crucifix's trance. She placed the blood-soaked crucifix back around her neck, staining her skin and gown in the process, but she didn't even flinch as the cold, wet gold touched her.

'Without looking at me, she barked at me that I knew what to do, so I dragged the trunk from the room, leaving Sister Nora alone with the crucifix. After I disposed of the trunk in the back garden, I went through all the rooms in the orphanage, collecting photographs, drawings and admission files, anything at all which contained her name. I burned them all that very night in the glowing embers that were left in the fire in my chambers.'

Katherine snorted. It was clear she didn't care for his pitiful excuses. She leaned closer to the ground to get a better view of the injured bee. 'I won't be leaving this bee alone, Father Michael. You know that no one, including this little bee here, ever truly leaves this place?' she said, echoing Sister Nora's initial warning to her. 'I'm just ensuring it stays here like the rest of us.'

Father Michael dropped his head in defeat. There was no getting through to Katherine. She refused to see reason. How could he make her see that she was following the same path as Sister Nora? He placed one hand on the statue of Mary and leaned into it to help himself get back to his feet. He dusted the knees of his pants and looked at Katherine in despair. 'Please, my child,' he begged. 'You are not like her. You do not have the crucifix. Do not give her the power to change you. For everyone's sake.'

'How dare you!' she snapped. 'After everything you have done, yet you preach about the supposed darkness within *me*. I do believe it was you, Father Michael, who so aptly advised that I was marked and being targeted, was it not? Is it any wonder that I have changed after all of that? I do not need your help or your concern. You're wasting your time even speaking with me. It would be better to use your time to prepare for your next sermon.'

He sighed. 'I will pray for you, dear Katherine,' he murmured, and shuffled off towards his quarters just as the heavens opened and the rain started pouring down. He glanced behind him one more time at the girl who was willing to choose a path of immense evil. She hadn't moved an inch, even though the rain was soaking her. Instead, she continued her sadistic entrapment of the defenceless bee.

Father Michael wiped away the tear that was threatening to spill down his face and returned to the main building. He had a sinking feeling that history was about to repeat itself, and he didn't have any idea how to stop it. The only thing he could do now was pray to the God almighty to save the souls of those who would be affected by the turmoil created by the shifting balance of the powers of darkness.

Katherine waited until she heard the soft thud of the convent's front door closing before she looked up again. She couldn't stop the laughter that tumbled from her mouth. What a foolish man. She didn't care for his little speech, although it had been a nice touch that he had been so honest about the Jane situation. There was no darkness manifesting inside her, attempting to control her. She was well within her senses; she was nothing at all like Sister Nora.

In fact, she was far worse. However, he had said one thing which stuck in her throat like sandpaper. 'You don't have the crucifix.' If he only knew her plan, he'd be quivering in fear. It was true that she didn't have the crucifix … yet. It was the key to taking everything from Sister Nora and destroying her.

Father Michael was right about one thing, though; she wasn't going to allow Sister Nora's power to change her. In fact, she wasn't going to give Sister Nora any power at all. She was going to take it for herself.

A droplet of rain fell on the bridge of her nose. She looked up at the sky and let out a delighted shriek. She would tackle Sister Nora tonight! With the weather deteriorating, it would be the perfect night to act; no one would hear her movements over the cracking of the thunder.

After all, Sister Nora couldn't be completely surprised by the turn of events that was going to happen. It was she who had told her that there was darkness within her. Katherine smiled as she thought, *If only my mother could see me now.* How would she have reacted to knowing that she was right all along – that her daughter truly did have a sinister side? Would she be petrified? Would she have sought help from the local priest to try to banish the evil within her? Katherine kicked the ground, dislodging the raindrops from the blades of grass as she imagined her dear mother's shock if she had known what Katherine had in store for the cursed nun.

She heard a faint buzz that pulled her from her distracted thoughts, and searched the ground. For a moment, she had forgotten about the injured bee lying victim in the grass. A parade of red ants had started to close in on the bee, waiting for the opportune moment to attack, when it was at its most vulnerable. Katherine tilted her head to the side and watched in twisted admiration as they circled around their prey. The bee was destined to die alone and in pain, at the mercy of whatever larger insect happened to come along. She thought it oddly poetic that the tiny ants circling the bee, threatening to consume it, were so much smaller than their victim. It was as if she was watching her own story play out in front of her and how she would overcome Sister Nora. She smiled again before crouching down to pluck the legs off the bee, hindering it from escaping and ensuring its demise.

She jumped up and wiped her hands on her dress, then walked towards her dorm room with a newfound pep in her step, just as the red ants started to descend upon the bee.

138

XXV

The earlier rain of the day had given way to a torrential thunderstorm. Katherine couldn't remember the last time she had seen weather this bad. The grounds were beginning to flood, and all outdoor chores were suspended as Sister Nora didn't want any unnecessary mud being dragged through the hallways. The orphans were given a supper of stale bread and curdling milk and were sent to bed. They all made their way up the creaky wooden stairs towards their bedrooms with only the flickering glow of candlelight to guide them as they went.

Katherine marched into her room and gazed out her window at the chaotic weather raging outside. Some of the girls were anxious about the thunderstorm, but Katherine welcomed the raucous claps of thunder and lightning with open arms.

Sister Nora would be doing her rounds soon, so Katherine picked up her rosary beads in preparation for her nightly prayers. But as she was about to kneel down, a thought surfaced. Why was she persisting with Sister Nora's tiresome routine? She was only a few hours away from having the ability to control everyone around her, of being in total control of her own life, so why waste time playing the submissive pawn?

She scolded herself and threw the rosary beads across the room. They landed with a soft thud and rattled across the floor. They were probably broken, but this didn't bother her in the slightest. She strode over to her bed, hitched up her nightdress and sat cross-legged on the mattress, staring at the slit in the door, willing Sister Nora to hurry up and begin her rounds.

At last, despite the rumbling of the storm, she heard the unmistakable sound of Sister Nora's heels striking the floorboards and door hatches being opened and shut. Katherine held her breath in anticipation as the footsteps grew closer and closer to her room, then halted. She squinted at the gap underneath her door and recognised the shadow of Sister Nora's feet.

Katherine whipped her head up just as Sister Nora flung open the hatch on her door. It took Katherine a few seconds for her eyes to adjust to the brightness of the candlelight, but once they had, she stared boldly at the nun. She tilted her head and sneered at Sister Nora, inviting her to chastise her. But she must have caught the nun off guard, because her eyes widened in shock as she peered into the room. They held each other's gaze for a few seconds before Sister Nora snapped her head back and slammed the hatch shut. Katherine could've sworn she heard the woman growl in frustration.

Katherine grinned as the sound of Sister Nora's footsteps grew fainter. Oh, how she had enjoyed the look of fear she had glimpsed in the nun's eyes! It was the first time she had ever retreated from Katherine, rather than reaching for the crucifix hanging on her neck. Katherine felt powerful and in control, and she couldn't wait to embody that feeling every day.

A flash of lightning brought Katherine back to the present moment. A thrill of excitement coursed through her – only a few more hours to go before she could spring into action.

She waited, lying on the dusty floorboards, her ear pressed firmly against them, waiting for the familiar hum of the organ to begin playing. It wasn't long before she could feel the vibration against the palms of her hands. That was her cue to begin.

She shoved her bedframe aside and retrieved the wire she'd hidden. Catching sight of the Judas carving in the wood, she laughed like a hyena. It was so ironic to think, that only a few weeks ago, she had detested being associated with Judas, but now she fully embraced the idea, accepting that she didn't have to hide that part of herself anymore.

She fiddled with the wire until she heard the familiar click of the lock opening. Swinging the door open, she took a deep breath and stepped out into the hallway on shaky legs. A combination of nerves and excitement was making her jittery. She tossed the wire back into her room and strutted down the hallway, without closing the door behind her. There was no need to fear the wrath of the nuns anymore. They would learn to fear her by the time dawn rose. Her heart beat so fast, she thought it might burst through her chest at any moment.

Katherine began to sprint towards the direction of the chapel. Her breathing became ragged, and she stumbled once or twice on the freezing-cold floors. She cursed herself for not putting on her shoes before she left her room. No doubt, her feet would be grazed and cut by the end of the night. There were no candles alight in the orphanage as they had all been snuffed out earlier when the nuns had retired to bed. Katherine had to rely solely on the sporadic flash of light coming through the windows from the lightning to guide her.

As she neared the heavy chapel doors, her ears had begun to ring, and adrenaline was coursing through her body. With every step she took, the vibration and the hum of the organ grew louder. She skidded to a stop and placed her quivering palms on the doors, then rested her head between them. This was it. This was her moment. Everything was about to change.

She would no longer be subjected to the vindictive abuse from that evil woman.

Katherine's plan was simple. She would use the element of surprise to her advantage. Sister Nora wouldn't be expecting anyone to intrude and, if she moved fast enough, Katherine was sure she could overpower her and rip the crucifix from her neck. She expected a struggle; Sister Nora wouldn't part willingly with the crucifix, but Katherine was prepared to do whatever was necessary to obtain what she felt was rightfully hers, even if it meant ending Sister Nora's life in the process. However, she hoped to avoid that. She wanted the nun alive so *she* could live in fear of her and her capabilities. Katherine would be in complete control – able to exact revenge for Nora's treatment of the orphans. It was what she deserved. She deserved to live under the shroud of a menacing figure, just as they had.

How would Sister Nora react to her intrusion? Would she be surprised by Katherine's retaliation or scared? Would she beg for mercy just as the dead orphans had done with her and mimic their desperate cries? A shudder of excitement raced through her and, taking a deep breath, she burst through the doors, a huge grin adorning her face. But as soon as she stepped across the threshold, her smile faltered. All her anticipation came crashing down. There was no one there. The chapel was empty, illuminated only by the moonlight shining in through the stained-glass windows. The organ was covered with an old sheet with no evidence of it having been used since Father Michael's service earlier that evening.

Katherine was utterly astonished. What was going on? *This is surely just a bad dream*, Katherine thought.

She inspected each pew as if, by some miracle, she would find an answer to the mystery. Perhaps someone had been playing a trick on her. Was this just another one of Sister Nora's cruel mind games?

Did she know I was coming? thought Katherine.

She spun around in disbelief. She had spent so long plotting and anticipating the moment when she would take back control of her life and gain all that power. She hadn't even considered what her next step would be if her grand plan failed.

The hairs on the back of her neck stood up. She broke into a cold sweat as she shuffled up to the altar. She passed by the open Bible at the pulpit, her fingers running over the wood as she walked closer. Ordinarily, she wouldn't have cared to even give the pages a second glance, but some of the words stood out to her, flashing like a beacon and inviting her to give the page a closer inspection.

She realised that this wasn't the usual Bible that Father Michael would have read from during his sermons. The frayed pages and the thick dust gathering in the spine indicated that it must have been quite old. She blew on the pages to get rid of the excess dust and let out a deep cough as the musty cloud settled again.

The Gospel of Luke was hidden beneath the shroud of smut in faded black words. There was one sentence which had been circled multiple times and underlined with black ink.

'Then Satan entered Judas.'

Katherine scoffed to herself. How fitting it was that this should be the prime sentence on the page. Her eyes scrolled down the rest of the page, her finger following the words as she read them. When she reached the end of the page, she noticed the sheet was puckered, as though something was behind it. She turned it over, and her eyes widened in shock. Someone had defiled the Bible and now it was splattered with ink. The entire page of text had been written over with words that chilled her soul. 'You have the Devil inside you. You are marked.'

Katherine slammed the Bible shut and stepped back, knocking over a candelabra. The sound of the brass hitting the marble floor echoed through the empty chapel. It was no coincidence that she should come face to face with text of such magnitude. That statement had been thrown in her face since the day she first arrived at the orphanage.

She'd been correct. Someone had deliberately set her up. She raised her arms to grasp her head and groaned in frustration. As she threw her head back, she noticed a strange shadow suddenly move in the gallery above.

She squinted and the shadow gradually came into focus. A woman was moving towards the centre of the gallery and, as she reached out to grip the brass railing, something glinted and her whole face came into view. Of course, it was Sister Nora, dark eyes alight with malice and that vile smirk on her face as she peered down at Katherine.

Consumed with anger and her desire to enact her plan, Katherine hastily moved towards the gallery, fully prepared to do whatever it took to get that crucifix. She charged towards the altar steps but, feeling faint, she stopped, gripping the nearby pew to steady herself. She glared up at Sister Nora, but she had gone.

All Katherine could hear was her own staggered breathing. 'One … two … three … four … five,' she counted under her breath. She had to remain calm and push past the unsteadiness. She just needed a few seconds to focus.

Where did she go? she wondered.

Still gripping the pew, she squinted into the darkness, just as a voice emerged from the shadows behind her.

'You still haven't learned. Nothing happens within these walls without me knowing. I know everything. I've been watching you for the last few weeks. I've seen the blazing desire in your eyes. I know what you want,' Sister Nora said. She laughed and shoved Katherine further into the pew. Katherine, already wobbly, toppled over and fell to the floor.

This wasn't how she imagined her plan would unfold. She had gone over every possible outcome, but none had included ending up at the mercy of Sister Nora. She kicked her legs, trying to wriggle out of Sister Nora's reach, but the nun grabbed her leg mid-kick and pulled her back towards the altar.

'Let me go!' Katherine shouted. She tried to grab hold of anything solid to halt her capture, but it was no use. The madwoman had her in a trap. But she wasn't willing to give up without a fight. If Sister Nora was intending to end her life, she wouldn't make it easy for her. Katherine's body felt heavy, her limbs refusing to respond to her desperate will to fight back.

'Since the very first moment I lay eyes on you, I knew you were trouble. Lurking around corners and trying to weasel your way into things that you have no business being a part of. You,' she said, while tilting her head towards the cemetery, 'are just as disposable as they are.

'What did you think you could achieve? That you'd take my crucifix for yourself? Free the oppressed children and allow them into the light? Restore the convent to its former glory?' she said. 'No. You see Katherine, I don't believe that. It was blatantly obvious that you wanted the crucifix for yourself, but you don't *really* care about what happens to the other children. I know you, and I know what lies are concealed within your soul.' Sister Nora jabbed a finger at her.

'You just want the power to fuel your own dark desires. You want to be the one in control. Well, I'm sorry to inform you, that won't be possible, and, just as you don't care about the others, they don't care about you. I'm certain they won't be whispering amongst themselves when you fail to appear tomorrow morning.'

Distraught, Katherine looked around wildly in a futile attempt to find something to use for protection. She turned back and her eyes widened as Sister Nora seized the chalice from the altar above and held it aloft.

Katherine threw her arms up to protect her face, just as the double doors of the chapel burst open. She heard two sets of footsteps running up the aisle. Sister Nora, consumed with her rage, was oblivious to the interruption. She raised the chalice higher and struck it against Katherine's head.

Katherine screamed out in pain and brought her hands down to cradle her now pulsing skull. Her heart felt like it was beating in her ears. Gingerly, she removed one hand. It was covered in blood.

Sister Nora grinned, a maniacal glint in her eye as she prepared to deliver another blow. Suddenly, the chalice clattered to the floor and the nun was dragged away, kicking and screaming.

Still struggling with the pain in her head, Katherine rolled over sluggishly onto her forearms.

'Get up, Katherine! There's no time!' a voice said.

It took a few seconds for Katherine's eyes to steady before she recognised Grace and Lauren as the two people who had pulled Sister Nora away from her.

'We heard the shouting from our room,' Lauren said. 'We knew it must have been you, and we wanted to help. We've spent too long being afraid of her.'

Sister Nora was struggling to reach Katherine with the vice grip that Lauren and Grace had on her arms. Her anger was boiling over and froth was beginning to form at the corners of her mouth. 'Just as well we came when we did,' said Grace, smirking, 'otherwise your head would have ended up looking worse than mine.'

Despite her pain, Katherine couldn't help but chuckle, even though the movement hurt her head more. Sister Nora was wrong; the orphans did care for each other here, or, at the very least, they cared enough to unite against their tormentor when it mattered most.

Katherine staggered to her feet and weighed up her options. The blood from her head dripped onto the white marble steps beneath her. Sister Nora was struggling to free herself from the vice-like grip that both girls had on her arms. Her black eyes were frenzied, and she was foaming at the mouth like a rabid animal. Her hysterical shrieks resounded through the chapel. If she were to get loose, Katherine dreaded the terrible repercussions for all of them.

They won't be able to hold her for long, Katherine thought. She had to act fast.

Katherine marched up the steps just as Sister Nora managed to snatch her arm away from Grace. With one arm free and a force unlike any other, she pushed Grace into the lectern, causing her to stumble headfirst into a pillar before her body rolled down the steps. Her head cracked as it collided with the floor.

'No!' Lauren screamed as she released her grip on Nora and rushed towards her lifeless friend. A dark crimson stream of blood was beginning to pool around Grace's head, the metallic smell filling the air. 'What have you done? Grace, wake up! Come on, wake up!' She shook Grace's body.

Sister Nora stalked towards Lauren as she wailed over Grace. With her back now towards Katherine, this was her opportunity. She charged at Sister Nora, shouldering her out of Lauren's pathway and knocking her to the ground. Katherine faltered. The pain in her head was making her dizzy but this small win gave her the impulse to carry on.

She spied the chalice lying where it had fallen from Sister Nora's murderous clutches just minutes before. As the nun struggled back to her feet, Katherine grabbed it and pounded it against her head, just as she had done to her. The shock of the initial impact brought Sister Nora down to her knees. Katherine's mind flashed back to past images of beatings in the nun's office, the pain and isolation, and the tender moments she had spent with Sister Sorcha, who had been so cruelly taken from her.

Fuelled by an insurmountable rage, she raised the chalice again. She couldn't let her live now. Sister Nora would never submit to her, so vengeance was the only option. She crashed the chalice against her head over and over again, each blow growing stronger as the adrenaline pulsed through her body. Sister Nora's body grew weak, and her eyes started to flutter shut. Throwing the chalice to one side, Katherine used both of her hands and wrapped them around Sister Nora's neck, squeezing so hard that bruises started to form beneath her fingertips. The nun's eyes bulged from the pressure and her hands became limp.

Katherine suddenly dropped her hands from Sister Nora's neck, allowing her to collapse in a heap on the altar. She couldn't let her die just yet; she had to witness Katherine's triumph over her former oppressor, understand that she was no longer in control. It had to be the very last thing she saw before she died.

Katherine leaned over Sister Nora's dying body and smirked. 'Looks like I'm the one in control now,' she said as she ripped the crucifix from the woman's neck and placed it around her own.

Finally, she thought. The gold chain was now resting comfortably against her chest, where it belonged. She closed her eyes and smiled in pure bliss.

She glanced down at the woman beneath her. 'I'm now the only God within these walls. I won!'

Despite only a whisper of life remaining in Sister Nora's body, she reached a shaking arm towards the crucifix that had been taken from her. Even in her final moments, the power of the crucifix was calling out to her. But her injuries were too severe and, with a final shudder, she dropped her arm to the floor and her head rolled to one side as she finally succumbed to Katherine's revenge.

Sister Nora's death brought a heavy silence to the chapel. The only sounds came from Lauren as she sobbed, mourning the loss of her friend.

Katherine glanced over at them. She was sorry that Grace had died. Both girls had gone out of their way to help her. Had it not been for their intrusion, she most likely would not have succeeded. However, she couldn't allow the pity she felt to distract her.

'She's gone, Lauren,' Katherine said as she approached the grieving girl. 'Let her rest. There's nothing more you can do for her now.' She placed what she thought was a comforting hand upon Lauren's shoulder and guided her away from the sickening scene in front of her. 'Grace said once that the lucky ones are those who leave this place. She's one of the lucky ones now. Try to focus on that.'

'What are you talking about, Katherine? Sister Nora is gone now. She can't hurt anyone anymore,' Lauren said, sniffling and wiping her nose on her sleeve. 'Grace didn't have to die. You have the crucifix now. Things would have been different for Grace if she'd lived. She wouldn't have to be afraid of her anymore.'

Katherine dropped her hand from Lauren's shoulder and straightened her back, thinking, *Things are going to be different, sure, but I wouldn't say you have nothing to fear anymore.*

Lauren must have sensed foreboding in Katherine's silence because she raised her head and said, 'Katherine … what's going on?'

Lauren backed away slowly, but Katherine only smiled at the girl. 'Nothing is going on, Lauren. You're right. Things are going to be different from now on. Grace is gone, but you don't have to be afraid. I'll handle this mess. Look, you've been through a great ordeal tonight, so you need to rest. Head back to the dorm, and do not utter a word of what took place tonight to anyone. They won't understand,' she said with a forceful tone.

Lauren nodded, but her expression was guarded. Katherine knew the girl didn't believe her.

Lauren stared at the crucifix resting against Katherine's chest and retreated further, eyes wide with fear and never leaving Katherine's figure until she reached the doors of the chapel. With a fumbling hand, she managed to push them open just enough to slip through them and bolt back to her dorm.

Katherine sighed. *She's going to be a problem. I'll need to take care of her eventually, but not now. I'll leave her to stew in her fear until it consumes her. It'll be more fun that way*, she thought.

Katherine sat down on the bloody altar steps and raised her hand to her head. The pain had started to subside, but she would be left with a nasty scar, an eternal reminder of what she had done … of what she *could* do. Her gaze rested on the two bodies, and she felt nothing. Sister Nora got what she deserved, and Grace had been collateral damage. Despite what Lauren thought, Grace *was* one of the lucky ones. She would never have been able to survive what was to come.

Reaching for the crucifix, Katherine clasped it tight against her chest. She started to rock back and forth as she burst out laughing, the sound echoing throughout the chapel.

'Yes. I will take care of things here,' she said. 'Nothing is going to get in my way now.'

151

XXVI

1873

The horse and trap once again rounded the corner and pulled up slowly at the main doors of the orphanage, the sound of the horse's hooves signifying the arrival of another orphan to the Convent of Mercy. The young, terrified orphan with her little bundle trudged up the steep steps to wait for whoever was in charge to guide her where to go. As she reached the top step, a figure emerged from the long, dark hallway behind the main doors.

This must be the Reverend Mother, she thought.

The nun's low black heels clicked on the stones as she approached the girl. An ornate gold crucifix hanging from her neck swayed into view.

'Welcome, child. I'm Sister Katherine.'

Epilogue

'So, you see, kid, she didn't just "kill a few kids", as you so *kindly* put it. She destroyed herself and her entire humanity to get the crucifix and the power it held. She was possessed. There's no other logical explanation for it. No woman of God would have done the things she did, committed such enormous atrocities, if she wasn't under the control of a dark force. And that, everybody, is the reason why we are all here tonight,' the tour guide said, clasping his hands together. 'To walk in the footsteps of evil and understand what life was like for those poor orphans, all those years ago, some of whom suffered a fate far worse than death.' He glanced at his wristwatch. 'Have a look around, get a feel for the place, and we'll meet back at the end of the stairs in, let's say, ten minutes?'

Some of the group flocked towards the end of the hallway, eager to see as much of the dormitory as possible, given their small window of time. Malcolm withdrew and hung back from the rest of the group. He didn't care to look deeper into the lives of some nuns who had lived and died long before his time. However, the story of Sister Katherine had intrigued him more than he was willing to admit, so he decided to take a quick walk about her room. He waited until the group had moved away, so he could inspect the notorious nun's room on his own. He couldn't risk his mother seeing him. If she thought he was showing the slightest interest in the whole fiasco, he would be stuck listening to her ramble on forever.

He scanned the bare room in front of him. It wasn't what he'd expected. He'd heard that if you stepped into a space where evil had resided, where brutal acts were carried out, you would feel an ominous sensation in the room, as if the perpetrator was still there, watching your every move. But this just felt like any other empty, dusty room. He was a little bit disappointed.

He kicked his boot on one of the deep groves embedded in the floorboards, stirring up some ancient smut in the process, and took a turn about the room. He was disillusioned when he didn't find any mysterious items. He looked out through the cracked window and saw the old graveyard outside. He shuddered, imagining how creepy it would have been to sleep so near to dead, rotting people.

Malcolm sat down on the creaky little bed and cracked his knuckles while he thought about the tale he'd just heard. If the graveyard part had been true, then what else had the tour guide been truthful about?

He stood up and, as quietly as he could, pushed aside the bed. To his surprise, there lay the carvings of the silver coins that had been given to Judas and that Sister Katherine had been marked with. Malcolm glanced at the door, wondering if his mother had noticed his absence. He tiptoed to the door and gently pushed it a little to conceal his snooping, then kneeled by the bed to get a closer look at the markings. They were quite faded, but there was no mistaking them. The markings were real. Curious, he ran his fingers over the circular symbols. As soon as his fingertips touched the etching, a shudder ran through his body, and he suddenly felt as if a large weight had settled itself on his back.

A vicious gust of wind swirled through the cracked window, forcing the bedroom door to click shut. Malcolm jumped. With the door fully closed, the room was beginning to feel more sinister, and he took this as his cue to leave. He moved the bed back to its original place and hurried to the door, eager to get as far away from the place as possible. But when he tried to open it, the door wouldn't budge.

He was about to call out for help, when he stopped short. A dull, raspy voice was whispering his name. The hairs on the back of his neck stood up, and his eyes widened in fear. He turned around slowly, afraid of what he might see, and rested his back flush against the door. His eyes darted nervously around the room, trying to make sense of where the voice was coming from. Finding no obvious answer, he decided his mind had been playing tricks on him. But then, the voice whispered his name again, so clearly this time, there was no doubt, something was speaking to him.

'The sill,' the eager voice whispered to him.

He gulped and, wondering if he was going crazy and because he couldn't get the door open anyway, he shuffled over to the windowsill to see if anything would happen. There was nothing out of the ordinary about the sill, but he knocked gently against the wood. The empty sound indicated the sill was hollow. He frowned, noticing a small gap in the architrave, inserted his fingers in it and pulled. The wood, caked in cobwebs, came away. He leaned it against the wall and peered inside the hole which was serving as a small storage space.

Much to his disappointment, he found nothing of significance hidden in the space, just some old, faded prayer books and a string of rosary beads which had been wrapped up in a muslin bag decorated with a cross. He examined the space again, amazed at how deep it was, and came across a dirty piece of cloth, yellow with age, that was securely tied with a piece of string. He pulled it out and felt a strange sensation – like a strong urge to pull the string open as if his life depended on it.

He fumbled with the tight bow, opening the cloth and revealing an object that tumbled straight into his awaiting hand. He raised his eyebrows as he shook his head. Nestled in his hands was the notorious crucifix the guide had said was responsible for the reign of terror at the orphanage, the relic that both paranormal experts and the Church had desperately sought for so long. And it had been found by him, a boy who hadn't even known about the orphanage's dark past until a few hours ago. He held the crucifix up by the gold chain, the ornate gold gleaming and glistening as if it were brand new.

'Malcolm! Where are you?'

Malcolm jumped at the sound of his mother's shrill voice, and he quickly tossed the piece of string and the cloth back into the secret space. He placed the missing piece of timber back in its place but kept a tight grip on the crucifix. No one could know what he had found. He intended to keep it for himself. Why would the voice reveal its hiding place, if it wasn't meant to belong to him? He relished the idea of what he could do if he possessed the power of the crucifix.

The bedroom door swung open, just as he dropped the crucifix safely in his pocket.

'What the hell are you doing? Come on, we're all heading back downstairs,' his mother snapped at him.

Malcolm rolled his eyes as he skulked out the door. If she only knew what he had found, she wouldn't dare to speak to him like that.

He made his way downstairs to join the rest of the group, stopping on the last step to place the stolen crucifix around his neck.

'Malcolm!' his mother shouted again from the entry hall ahead of him.

His face darkened at her incessant nagging. He didn't need to listen to her giving out to him anymore. He bypassed the rest of the group and strode out the main door of the orphanage, ignoring the rain that was pouring down. He leaned against the decaying statue in front of the building, stroking the crucifix in awe. Looking up, he marvelled at a bright flash of lightning in the sky as he clutched the crucifix to his chest and smiled.

Why wait? he thought.

He had received enough scolding after his latest suspension to last him a lifetime. Everyone treated him like an outcast, even his own mother. So why wait to make her feel sorry for her actions when he could just act right now. A shame for the rest of the group, maybe. They hadn't done anything to hurt him but, then again, they were all ridiculous fanatics, and one really shouldn't go looking for evil. They would all be sorry. He smiled broadly and strode back to the main building, slamming the door shut behind him.

An eerie silence descended upon the grounds just before the screaming began from within.